CW00392854

The Condottiero

(A Tudor Deceit)

by

Anne Stevens

Tudor Crimes Book IV

TightCircle Publications

Foreword

It is October 1531, and two great power bases are struggling to sway King Henry, in the matter of his divorce. The king sways from his Lord Chancellor, Sir Thomas More to his Privy Councillor, Thomas Cromwell, like a willow, bending in the breeze.

Lady Anne Boleyn grows impatient, and is pressing Henry to bring things to a head. She would have More put aside, and her new favourite, Thomas Cromwell put in charge. Henry agrees, but still vacillates, hoping for a miraculous change of heart by Pope Clement in Rome.

In a bid to end the seeming deadlock, Cromwell suggests sending more emissaries to meet with the principle lords in Padua, Venice, Milan, and Rome, knowing that their efforts will be in vain.

Along with the new missions, Thomas Cromwell decides to send his own, with a specific agenda. Will Draper and his confederates are tasked to do but one thing: hurry the Pope into a swift refusal.

Despite having travel documents, and the support of a powerful master, Draper knows he must face a new world of intrigue. The French king covets Milan, as does Venice and Padua, and the Pope wants a good marriage for his son. Deals are made, and promises broken, as each state vies to win out, and emerge all powerful in a disjointed Italy.

It is Will Draper's duty to escort England's ambassador at large, the poet Thomas Wyatt, to Rome, and somehow, get him an audience with Pope Clement. Despite having served in Ireland, and fought Welsh rebels, Draper is in for a rude awakening. The city states of Italy seem to be small, oasis's of calm, in a sea of carnage and ruin, but appearances can be deceptive.

In a time when five thousand men, and a few canon, can make you a prince, the great mercenary warlords, known as condottieri, are poised to change the map of Italy forever. The greatest condottiero of them all is Malatesta Il Baglioni, and his belligerent desires, ultimately, must come into direct conflict with the Englishmen's own aims.

The road to Rome is a difficult one. If Draper and Tom Wyatt are to return, alive, they must face savage conflict, dangerous intrigue, and horrendous natural calamity.

1   At Court

"Any news, Master Cromwell?" Miriam has asked the same for the last week. She is without her husband, Will Draper, and her brother Moshe, who they all call Mush at Austin Friars, to hide the young man's Jewish birth. Cromwell, smiles at the girl, for unlike the previous days, he does have something to tell her.

Cromwell's nephew, Richard, the poet, Thomas Wyatt, Will Draper, and Mush, his brother -in- law, who has recently taken Will's family name, sailed from Plymouth eleven days before, in the king's ship 'The Sovereign', bound for Bilbao, in northern Spain. From there, they must travel across country to Girona, where another ship, a Flemish trader, part owned by Cromwell, waits to take them on to Genoa. From there, they will ride to Venice.

The big, four-masted carrack, a converted merchantman, has made good time, and Thomas Cromwell has just had news of its safe return to Plymouth Hoe. He smiles at the girl, who is so like a daughter to him, and holds up a report.

"They are all very well, my dear," he says to her. "The ship's captain is in my pay, and writes to inform me that Will, Richard, Mush, and Master Wyatt, were landed safely at Bilbao. They have diplomatic safe conducts, recognised by the Emperor Charles' people, and by now, they should be in Girona, or even at sea again."

"So many boats," Miriam mutters, touching the beautiful gold star at her neck. "Could they not have rather ridden, Master Tom?"

"Twelve, or thirteen hundred miles, across the most dangerous, and unfriendly country," Cromwell replies. "Having to face constant border crossings, bandits, outlaws, and roving bands of unpaid mercenaries, is not my idea of a safer passage, my dear Miriam. Even with fresh horses waiting at every stop, they would scarcely have done it in less than twenty five, or thirty days, and under constant fear of attack."

"It is a poor choice you give my man, and my brother," Miriam says. It is the closest to a reproach that she can bring herself to make to her benefactor. "At least, they will be in Italy, before the winter sets in."

"How are things with you, my dear girl?" Eustace Chapuys appears at the gate, with two servants in tow. "And good day to you, Thomas. Are you venturing out today?"

"Of course I am, you silver

tongued little rogue," Thomas Cromwell replies. "Today is a special occasion, is it not?"

"Is it your birthday, Master Eustace?" Miriam asks. "Had I known, I would have…"

"No, no, my dear, calm yourself," the little Savoyard says, preening in his new doublet, and with yet another monstrous hat on his head. "Today, is special. His Majesty, after almost three years, has invited me to an audience, at Whitehall Palace."

"You have met the king before, though," Miriam replies. "Why is this time any different?"

"Politics," Cromwell says, interrupting. "Chapuys, the man, is known to Henry, but Chapuys the Imperial ambassador is not yet formally accepted. Today, Henry will stop fencing him off, meet him, face to face, and accept his formal introduction. The king will put out his hand, for the ring to be kissed. It means that Henry is offering his hand to the Emperor Charles, in a gesture of love, and peace."

"And I am the conduit," Chapuys says. "I will be introduced, and bend my knee. Then I will beg him to take my passport, and accept my master's deepest felicitations."

"And presents too, I hope?" Chapuys beckons one of his men over and takes a box from him. He opens it, and displays a silver communion goblet.

"Hand chased by the greatest silversmith in all Christendom," he tells his friend. "There is not another like it in the world, and it cost Charles six thousand ducats. I shall present it to His Majesty, in person."

"In that hat?" Cromwell puts in, knowing it will annoy his friend. "Let me find you a less … flamboyant … cap, my friend. I fear that the feathers might tickle the king's nose, and he will sneeze on you. The gust might blow you back to Spain."

"Such a jester," Chapuys replies, happily. Today's action will confirm him as ambassador, and encourage the emperor to keep him in place. This is to his liking, as he has grown fond of his English friends, and there is little enough for him back home. "I thought we could walk to the palace together, and show the king how well we get along."

"A good idea. I believe I shall," Cromwell says. "Give me a moment, and I will have Rafe Sadler and Barnaby Fowler put on their best coats, and come along with us. The common people will cheer us, and shout when they see our grand parade ... if only at the sight of your wonderful hat."

"Curse it, Thomas, I will leave it behind, if you only hurry. I must not keep the king waiting."

The small, dignified ambassador, and his entourage of friends, set off for Whitehall, with Eustace Chapuys in the van. As they come to the front entrance, some professional loiterers raise a cheer, and one shouts out a rousing '*Gor' bless yer worship!*' The delighted Savoyard plucks a handful of copper coins from his purse, and distributes them into eager palms. Cromwell cannot help but smile, as he knows that Chapuys salary is always four months late, and amounts to only forty pounds a year.

Whilst this is enough to maintain a reasonable standard of living for most gentlemen of the court, it does not allow for the trappings of ambassadorial pomp, and leaves Chapuys out of pocket, time and again. Cromwell guides his friend past the rest of the begging hands.

"Leave some of them for Stephen Gardiner to give to, Eustace," he says. "Now he is made up to Bishop of Winchester, he has more than enough to throw about."

They are granted access, by deferential guards, warned that Chapuys' visit today is of a special nature, who bow, and rush to open inner doors. The vast reaches of Whitehall stretch out before them. The ambassador continues into the bowels of the great new palace, flanked by Cromwell, Rafe Sadler, Barnaby Fowler, and Chapuys' own two servants.

Apart from the many English gentlemen present there are dozens of visiting foreigners, who flood to Whitehall to pay their humble respects. Henry often enjoys meeting them, and is eager to hear news from the wider world. Each tall story is rewarded with a little gift, dependant on its amusement value.

Recently, great amusement was had, when an envoy from Muscovy, bedecked in strange furs, and with a beard, almost as big as his chest, mistook Sexton, the king's fool, for the king. To see the foreign lord bowing, and attempting to kiss the jester's hand caused Sexton to gambol about, posturing like the finest of the fine.

"Call me Hal," he had declared, and only returned to his usual grovelling respect, when the Duke of Norfolk kicked him up the backside. The Muscovite was soothed, and taken away to regain his composure.

Now, Thomas Cromwell pauses,

smiles, and nods towards three men clustered in one of the great, open gallery's numerous alcoves. He recognises two of them as the Venetian ambassador, Lodovico Falier, and Marco Raphael, who professes to be a teacher of languages, but is, in fact a Venetian agent, sent to pry into English business.

"Master Falier, my dear ambassador," Cromwell says, offering a small, sharp bow. "May I introduce Eustace Chapuys, the Holy Roman ambassador to this court?" The man gives a generous bow, and replies in Italian. Marco Raphael starts to interpret, but Cromwell says:

"*Tutti noi parliamo italiano, signore. E 'la lingua della poesia.*"

"That is true," the Venetian ambassador replies, in quite acceptable English. "Just as your language is the voice of commerce."

"I do not know this gentleman," says Cromwell. "Is he new to the court?"

"Forgive my manners, Master Cromwell," Falier says. "This is Mario Savorgnano, a fellow Venetian, who is here to tour your country … for pleasure."

"You must pay particular attention to our busy ports, my friend," Cromwell says, pointedly. "Where the king has sixty great men o'war. Our navy is quite the most powerful in the world now, save for the Ottoman infidels. Did you come here, straight from Venice, sir?"

"No, sir, I did not." Savorgnano pauses, then realises that Cromwell is, in a quiet way, demanding answers of him. "I quitted the Imperial Court, which is, as you know, in Brussels, and journeyed to Ghent, From there, I took a carriage, and visited Bruges."

"A handsome town, Master Savorgnano," Chapuys puts in, trying to hurry the conversation along. He is eager to meet with the king.

"Yes, sir, it is considered to be the handsomest, and most magnificent city of any in all of Flanders. It contains an infinite number of large palaces, inhabited by men of diverse nations, in which they carry on their mercantile traffic. Then there are houses without end, belonging to private gentlemen, part of which are by the water's side, with very handsome quays in front, with seats all made alike; and looking on the canals. I almost fancied myself to be back   at Venice."

"Then a fair wind blew you here?" Cromwell says. He smiles, but his eyes are asking what the man is really all about.

"A man can admire only so many

merchant's houses, and fine churches," the Venetian explains. "I took horse, and in one day arrived at Calais, a distance of some thirty miles."

"An English town," Chapuys says. "I recall it as being a most vulgar, and dirty place."

"It is a very strong place, as I will tell my master on my return. Your king guards the town well, for it is a true fortress, and gives you control of the channel. On that same night, two hours before daybreak, I embarked on board a small boat, and with a pleasant south-west wind, and a calm sea, crossed from Calais to England in just six hours."

"Then you saw Dover castle, and its great guns." Cromwell gestured all about himself, as if encompassing the four points of the compass. "Our island has the appearance of a fortress, sir. It is difficult to land anywhere, other than in the harbours. I hope you see Canterbury, and visit the cathedral. Saint Thomas Beckett's shrine is magnificent. It is ornamented with precious stones, and sundry jewels, and with so much gold that its value is inestimable. Then, you must go to Winchester. You know Master Gardiner, I suppose. As he once visited Venice."

"As did you, sir," the man

12

replies, "many years ago."

"Ask Stephen Gardiner what he thinks of an alliance between our two great seafaring states, Signor," Cromwell says. "He will tell you that Venice has more in common with England, than it does with Rome."

"Sir, you do my job for me," Savorgnano replies.

"Come sir, you must have something to pass on to your master," Thomas Cromwell tells him. "You must inform him that England is strong, and well able to hold its own. Tell him that Tom Cromwell tells you this."

"You see through me, sir," the stout Venetian says, smiling ruefully. "You must realise that I come as a friendly agent. The Doge wishes only to ensure that, if need be, England will fight on the right side."

"Forgive me, Master Cromwell," the Venetian ambassador puts in, "but this is neither the time, nor place to discuss such weighty matters."

"Then do not bring spies into the royal Court," Signor Falier," Cromwell says, softly. "We will speak again, Master Savorgnano. Come to me at Austin Friars."

Cromwell, much to Chapuys' relief continues the progression, leaving the bemused Venetians behind. The ambassador and his two spies look at one another, and shake their heads in dismay. How, Savorgnano muses, does the man know so much? He has the feeling that Cromwell knows every movement, and has been receiving news of his visit, since the day he left Padua.

He will write his report to the Venetian Senate, and tell them about the great, and accessible Thames, guarded by great fortresses, and huge galleons, twice the size of any other war ship he has ever seen. Then he will explain that the city is fast becoming the hub of a great commercial alliance, and is governed by merchants - men of real worth. All things considered, he will write, England is ruled well, and its capital city is a very rich, populous, and mercantile place, but not as beautiful as Venice.

Cromwell and Chapuys continue, nodding their way past the ambassadors of Rome, Milan, and France, who acknowledge, or ignore each other, as the dictates of that day's politics suggest. Later, they will all dine together, and exchange snippets of information.

"You rather shocked the Venetian ambassador," Chapuys mutters, smiling at some ladies, who curtsey back. "What was your purpose?"

"I dislike foreign spies," Cromwell says. "Even ones who report favourably to their masters. The Doge is a cautious fellow, and wants to reassure himself about the embassy I am sending to him."

"You mean to Rome," Chapuys says. "Ambassador Wyatt, and Will Draper, are to see the Pope, are they not?"

"Eventually," Cromwell says, amiably. "I thought they might visit Venice and Padua first, just to say hello."

"Just to say…but no, Thomas," Chapuys says. "What are you up to now?"

"Nothing, my friend," Cromwell says. "I did the Doge a great service once, and Captain Draper's visit will merely jog his memory."

"You wish a favour from him?" Chapuys asks, but Cromwell steps back, and lets the little Savoyard advance. His great moment is at hand, and Cromwell is pleased for his friend. Courtiers part, and create an avenue for him, leading to the king. Henry is in his finest regalia, and is standing on a small dais, to accentuate his higher position. It is hardly necessary in poor Chapuys case, who is a good foot shorter than the majestic King of England.

Behind, two trumpets flourish, and a herald announces him as Master Eustace Chapuys, the most exalted

Emperor Charles's ambassador to the English court. Every man's head bows low, and the ladies all execute a well rehearsed curtsy. One or two cast covetous eyes, for a rich foreigner is a good catch for a single girl, no matter his height, or his age.

"My Lord Ambassador!" Henry roars, and throws his arms wide. "You are most welcome." The king proffers his right hand, for the ring to be kissed in formal obeisance, and Chapuys bows, and presses his lips to the huge ruby. As he goes to rise, there is a sudden movement, and Lady Anne Boleyn is there, holding out her own ring hand to him.

"Welcome, Master Chapuys," she says, in her quite excellent French. The Savoyard is stricken with horror. For three years, he has avoided all contact with the Boleyn woman, and is under strict orders never to acknowledge her, in any way. He has nowhere to turn, without mortally offending the king, so takes the delicate little hand, and kisses the ring.

"Good day, my lady," Chapuys says, colouring up. It is the closest he has ever been to the woman, and cannot see what Henry finds so fascinating about her. "I did not know you were back in court."

"When I heard that my dearest Henry was going to receive you," she says, smiling, "I changed my plans, just to be here. Now, you must not be a stranger, sir. I expect to see you often at our balls. Is there a Mistress Chapuys?"

"Alas no, my lady," Chapuys says.

"I am sure we can find you a *mistress* or even two here, sir," Henry says, and there is a ripple of laughter at the king's clever play on words.

"I detest the state of bachelorhood, Monsieur Chapuys," Lady Anne tells him. She is happy with her little deception, and is enjoying the ambassador's unease. "You must come, and walk in the gardens with my ladies in waiting and I … some day."

"You are too kind, Lady Boleyn," Chapuys replies, and steps back, to be enfolded within the friendly arms of Thomas Cromwell and his young men.

"Well done, Eustace," Cromwell tells him. "You have healed a rift today, and your master will be proud of you."

"You did this to me," Chapuys says, sharply. "You led me to the block, like a lamb to the slaughter."

"Not I, sir," Cromwell says. "I came to give you support. The lady, as far as I knew, was at Westminster. Still, what harm is done? You have been introduced to Anne Boleyn. That does not mean you support her cause, or are turning into a protestant, does it?"

"No, it does not," Chapuys replies. "Though the emperor will see it differently."

"Not when he receives your next report." Cromwell is already thinking how best to turn the little setback into an advantage for both Chapuys, and himself. "In it, you will be able to tell him that you have infiltrated the Boleyn camp, and hope to pick up much vital information therein."

"The tittle tattle of ladies," says Chapuys.

"Not so," his friend tells him. "There will be certain facts, unknown outside their circle. For instance, you can hint at George Boleyn's obvious dislike for his wife. Jane, the Lady Rochford complains to me that her husband never fulfils his duties as a married man, and enjoys more peculiar pleasures."

"What?" Chapuys cannot believe his ears. "George Boleyn is a … *Quel est la mot*? … Sodamite?"

"Hush now, " Cromwell says. They are still strolling about the gallery. "Hint, my friend. Tell your master a little, then let the story run its course. After that, we might find out something about the Boleyn father. Perhaps he is a drunkard, or a wife beater? No, I know what it will be; I wager he is defrauding the king."

"My God, what are you saying?"

"Nothing out loud, Eustace," Cromwell says. "There are things that might need saying, but not by me. If the source of the gossip cannot be found… well, your position is secure, and we are all blameless."

"I see. You are a rogue, Thomas," Chapuys says. "Now, what do I do?"

"Wait for the dancing to start, then approach La Boleyn, and bring up the subject of Paris. She loves the damned place, and will enjoy talking to someone who knows the city well. In this way, she might reveal something interesting to you."

"Why do you help me so?"

"Is not friendship enough of a reason?" Cromwell asks.

"We are both too wise to think that, my friend." Chapuys strolls away, and starts to chat with one of the king's physicians, who accepts small tokens of friendship, in return for information.

The Doctor, Thomas Wendy, is just thirty years old, and the youngest of the king's medical men. As one of the court's four royal physicians, he is able to give an accurate insight as to Henry's current temperament, and state of health.

"You are well, Master Chapuys?" Wendy asks.

"I hope so, Doctor," Chapuys replies. "How is the king?"

"You do not ask me to divulge medical information about my patient, I trust?"

"Of course not," Chapuys says. "I enquire in only a general way, as one friend to another." Later, the ambassadors servant will pass a small purse to the doctors assistant, and honour will be satisfied.

"In that case, I can say that the king is… disquieted," Doctor Wendy tells him. "I fear his current abstinence from the pleasures of the flesh is to blame."

"The king needs a woman." Chapuys understands. "Perhaps if he was to be encouraged to … exercise himself in further directions?"

"I am sure that would suit you very well, my dear Master Chapuys," Doctor Wendy replies. He is not fond of the Boleyn clan either, and wishes that, should the king divorce, he does look further a field. Aside from taking Chapuys' presents, the good doctor is also receiving a small stipend from Cromwell, and agrees with him, that a nice German princess would be a perfect match. A few healthy Lutheran baby boys will lift the king's spirits beyond measure, and rid his mind of French raised sluts.

*

"Is that you, Thomas?" Henry calls. "Come here to me, Master Cromwell, I would have a word in your ear." The Privy Councillor obeys, smiling, and bowing.

"Yes, sire?"

"How goes my … matter?" Henry drops his voice, so that Anne does not hear. If it is good news, he will have the pleasure of telling her, and if it is bad, she best not know. Cromwell understands, and with a quiet 'may I' he steps closer to the king than it is normally fit to do.

"Excellent news," he whispers.

"Of the king's great matter?" The king's fool, Sexton, known as Patch, steps between the two men, and clutches his own private parts. "For it is truly great, Master Blacksmith."

"Away with you, Patch," the king says, but he is smiling at both the jest, and the compliment about his manhood. "Forgive my jester, Thomas, for he is a natural fool, and cannot make his tongue work with his brain."

"Fool am I?" Patch says, leering at the king. "I have free food, clean laundry, new shoes, and good ale, when ever I desire. Why sire, 'tis only the lack of a strumpet as makes us different!"

The king is going red in the face, as he perceives that it is now he who is the butt of this particular jest. Things look as though they might go ill with the simple minded jester, when Charles Brandon, Duke of Suffolk, takes him by the elbow, and pulls him away.

"Come, Master Patch, the ladies want to see you caper, and drool," he says. It is a wide held belief that those afflicted with a naturally simple mind, are endowed in other ways. Thus several of the court ladies have ventured into the fool's bed, where they discovered the truth of the old story, much to Patch's delight. "Who knows, perhaps one of them might *dance* with you?"

"I tire of that fool. Sometimes, I curse the day Cardinal Wolsey gave him to me. Damn, but I miss the man. Did I ever tell you how I was going to forgive him, Thomas?"

"Most gracious, sire. My report?"

"Oh, yes. Do go on."

"My people are reported well on the way. Wyatt and his company should be landing in Genoa soon. From there, they travel to Venice, and pay our respects to the Doge."

"He will fall in with our desires?" the king asks. "You seem so ... certain of it."

"I knew Andrea Gritti, over twenty years ago, sire," Cromwell explains. "He is favourably disposed towards me, and wishes nothing but friendship with Your Majesty." In truth, The current Doge of Venice owes everything to Thomas Cromwell. As a very young man, the Englishman travelled to Italy, in search of adventure, and found himself fighting on the losing side.

After the final, disastrous defeat, the young Cromwell is desperate to escape. He flees the carnage on horseback, then sees a wounded officer, staggering away from the battle field. The man is dazed, and easy prey for any victorious Spaniards who might come along. Cromwell cannot bring himself to abandon the wounded Venetian, so drags him up, and lays him across the horses withers.

The wounded man is called Andrea Gritti, and they return to Venice, where they become firm friends. Years later, as Thomas Cromwell runs the affairs of England, so Gritti is elected as the Doge, supreme head of the Venetian state.

"Then all goes well," Henry

says. "I will inform the Lady Anne. She will be most pleased with you, Thomas!"

The king goes off to ingratiate himself into the Boleyn good books, leaving Cromwell wondering at the risk he is taking. There is, he concludes, no other way. With Sir Thomas More still in the hunt, he must gain the advantage, and the only way to do that is to ruin the Lord Chancellor's own plans.

*

Stephen Gardiner, who Thomas Cromwell was trying to send to France, as the new ambassador, has been, without warning, made Bishop of Winchester by the king. This has created an unworkable triumvirate, with More working against Gardiner's influence with the king, and them both trying to alter his own plans.

Henry, in his wisdom, thinks that by playing off the three cleverest men in England against one another, he will achieve his own ends. Cromwell sighs at the naivety of the king's plan, for all he has done is create two obstacles for him to remove.

It is a source of great regret to Cromwell that the two enemies he must overcome, were once, his closest, and dearest friends. The next few months will be vital, he realises, and the outcome is dependent on the diplomatic skills of a

young poet, and the martial abilities of an
ex soldier.

2   The Dogado

"My God!" Will Draper cannot
believe how beautiful the city looks from

the high poop deck of the ship, sent to collect them from the mainland. "Have you ever seen anything so magnificent?"

"The Dogado, we call it," Signor Borello says, with great pride. "The city, and islands of Venice, ruled by the Doge and his Senate." His English is good, as is the man's French, and Latin. Once, he explains, it was his wish to serve the church.

"A pretty enough sight," Tom Wyatt says. He is still out of sorts from the journey, and finds it hard to enjoy the view. Mush and Richard Cromwell are dozing on the deck, in the early afternoon sunshine. The days at sea, and the hard ride from Genoa have taken their toll, and they must rest , if they are to be of any use to anyone.

It is the start of October. Back home, it will be like wintertime, but here, the weather is clement, and always warm against their northern European skins. Only Mush, with his olive complexion is truly comfortable with the heat. As he dozes, he can hear the Venetian's voice droning on, and decides that he does not like the man. He is boastful, and self seeking; a typical politician.

The ship, one of the fast Venetian coastal galleys slips into the harbour, and is tied fast by a swarm of small, dark skinned men, who proceed to unload the cargo. Borello ushers his charges onto the dock and conducts them through a short passage, where they come out into the Piazza San Marco. It is deliberately done, to awe new visitors with the splendour of the city.

Mush rubs his eyes open, and stares up at the vast campanile tower, and is almost made dizzy by the sight. Almost at once, other sights rush in, to stagger the senses. Thomas Wyatt whistles softly. The great basilica, the vast square, and the Doge's palace to the other side, will provide enough beauty for a hundred poems.

"Master Wyatt wishes to present his letters to the Doge, as soon as is convenient," Will says, aware that the spectacle is meant to put them in their place. "We have urgent business in Rome."

"This evening, Signor Draper," Borello tells him. "You must have powerful friends to obtain so speedy an audience with the Doge. Are you, perhaps the friend of your King Henry?"

"I am Thomas Cromwell's man," Will Draper replies. "We all are. He is the king's foremost advisor."

"He is?" Borello smiles, and nods. "Then the Lord Chancellor is out of favour?"

"Sir Thomas concerns himself with other than foreign affairs," Tom Wyatt puts in.

"More is a great friend of the church," the Venetian says.

"My delegation is authorised to negotiate with both the Pope, and your own master, Signor. May I ask your position, in relation to the Doge?"

"I am a Senator, of course," Borello says. "Not someone who would normally greet a party of travellers. As I say, you have influence. I hope that influence will not be brought to bear on our Doge. English interference in Venetian affairs will not be tolerated."

"Is that the opinion of the whole Senate, Signor Borello?" Will asks.

"Venice is an independent city state, sir," Borello replies, "and does not need foreign gold, or promises of support."

"With such an advocate as yourself," Tom Wyatt says, "I doubt any nation will wish to hold out the hand of friendship. Now, please show us to our quarters."

*

"I doubt you made a friend there," Richard says, after they are safely lodged in their rooms.

"Borello is a fool," Wyatt replies. He unbuckles his sword, and hangs it on a peg by the door. "Master Cromwell has schooled me well about those around the Doge. He tells me that a place in the Venetian Senate can be bought for two thousand ducats, so that, apart from a core of wise men, there are many merchants, money lenders and petty politicians, there because they can raise enough money for a bribe."

"Then we will be able to bribe Gritti," Will says.

"I doubt it," Wyatt tells them. Thomas Cromwell knows his man, and does not think he can be bribed in so open a way. "The bribes don't go to the Doge. They go to a central treasury, which controls its ledgers as well as a banking house. The Doge is the prime Senator, amongst a hundred, and has influence, but his power is not absolute."

"They need a king," Will says.

"Yes, and our king needs a son," Wyatt replies. "Barring a miracle, the only way that will happen, is if he remarries."

"There is always young Fitzroy," says Richard Cromwell.

"Never. England will not tolerate a bastard sitting on the throne" Will recalls the events of a few months earlier, when Baron Montagu almost managed to start a civil war over the child. "We must accomplish our aims."

"Why must we stop in Venice?" Mush asks, starting to wake up. "Let us rest, and ride on, tomorrow."

"Without a safe conduct from the Doge?" Wyatt shakes his head. "We would not last fifty miles, before every brigand in the Veneto descends on us. No, we must stay with the plan. Cromwell is sure the Doge will oblige us, and has entrusted letters to my keeping, which will sway him to our cause."

"I don't know about letters, but a huge bag of gold ducats might do the trick," Richard grumbles. "I wonder what the food is like here?"

*

Cromwell's massively built nephew need not have worried about his stomach. On the short walk to the Doge's palace there were food stalls every few steps. Richard stops at two or three, and spends four silver pennies, buying exotic delicacies, ready cooked, and demanding to be eaten.

"We are going to a banquet," Mush says, poking his friend's huge girth.

"There are banquets, and there are banquets," Richard replies, enigmatically, and shoves a whole sweet pastry into his mouth. More follow, and his chin and beard is soon matted with honey, and flecks of fine Madeira sugar. Venice is the gateway to the east, and the city uses luxuries like sugar, mace, cinnamon, salt, and black pepper as everyday condiments.

A crowd of Venetians are milling about outside the Doge's palace, each greeting the other with familiarity. Ordinary town's people can wander into the palace, and ask to see a senator or even the Doge, as they wish, and have more licence than any freeborn Englishman.

"Signor Gritti runs Venice like Master Cromwell runs Austin Friars," Mush says. "Look at the women!" The young man, recently betrothed to a beautiful Welsh girl called Gwen, is astounded by their beauty.

"English?" A thin, well dressed young man asks, and Mush nods, and asks him about the array of attractive women, sauntering about the great piazza. The man, introduces himself as Bartolommeo Rinaldi, the son of a merchant, and tries to explain in halting English.

"My Italian is good," Mush tells him, and the man grins in relief.

"I am glad of that, for my English is poor," he replies, and explains about the girls. "This country is very beautiful, and there are many pretty girls. They must either marry well, or come to Venice, as courtesans."

"Whores?" Mush says the English word, but his new friend shakes his head.

"No, not that, my English friend. You do not give these women a few coins for their favours. It is like this; No matter what their station is, they are all to be addressed, politely, as *Donna*. In the cooler part of the day, when the mosquitoes sleep, and fat husbands are in their counting houses, amorous gentlemen go out about the Piazza, or the smaller *Campos*, and saunter around, looking as wealthy as one can."

"Peacocks luring the hens," Mush says, with a smile.

"Just so. On meeting a woman in the street, you establish if she is a bored seeker after pleasure, or a *courtesan.*"

"And the difference?" Tom Wyatt asks. He is eager to speak with the Doge, but always has time to discuss the frailties of the female sex. "I recall the Roman courtesans being most mercenary."

"It is so the world over, sir," young Rinaldi replies, warming to the subject. "The courtesan will sniff out the rich men, and spurn the rest. You must seek out a bored wife, or a wayward daughter, and take her to a tavern. In Venice, all persons go without any reserve, to such places. The husband seldom takes things amiss, but often remains obliged to you, as he usually has his own mistress to visit. They often thank you, and if he sees you with her, he departs, so as not to cause any unseemliness."

"Do they expect presents?" Richard asks.

"Mere trifles for the *Donnas*, such as flowers, or some pretty ribbons for their hair," the young Venetian explains. "Though a courtesan will expect a jewel worth at least a hundred ducats."

"The women are all extremely handsome," Richard says, appreciatively. "How much is a hundred ducats, Will?"

"Almost thirty five pounds," Will replies, slapping his bear-like friend on the back. "You must find yourself a willing matron, Richard, for your uncle is not *that* generous."

"Do you have business with the Senate then?" Bartolommeo Rinaldi asks. He prefers to be with the younger set, and finds the ruling caste to be too old, and too boring. "Conclude it quickly, and I will take you all out."

"Our thanks," Tom Wyatt says,

wistfully, "but we cannot. We must dine with the Doge, and then conduct some diplomatic affairs. I fear it will be late before we are done."

"Another day then, my friends," the young man says. "Ask anyone where the palazzo of the Rinaldi family is, and they will direct you. I am at your service, day and night, gentlemen." He bows, and darts off, after a young, dark haired woman, who is fluttering a handkerchief in his direction.

"What a splendid way to spend every evening," Mush says, and they all laugh. A guard, idly checks their name against a list, and has a page boy lead them to the banqueting hall. As they stroll through the palace, they are dumb with awe, at the beauty of the décor, and wonder that they ever thought Austin Friars or Whitehall to be luxurious.

Three tables are laid out in a U shape, and there are about sixty place settings. Tom Wyatt cannot help but notice that the plates are not pewter, but silver, and that there is a matching knife and fork by each plate, together with a silver chased wine cup. Richard, who is his uncles nephew, after all, assesses each place setting to be worth twenty Thalers. He multiplies this by the number of settings, and guesses the table wear alone to be worth twelve hundred Thalers of silver.

"How much is a Thaler compared to a Ducat?" he asks Mush. The boy grins and shakes his head.

"Once more, I will explain," he says. "One Thaler weighs an ounce of silver, and is equal to two Ducats. A Ducat is a twelfth of an ounce of gold, and there are almost three of them to an English pound. So, twelve hundred Thalers is about eight hundred pounds."

"I wager they count each piece after dinner," Will tells his friend. "So don't get any ideas."

"I'm more interested in what they will put on the plates," Richard replies. "Where do we sit?" The tables are filling rapidly, but the elevated seat in the middle, and two places either side, remain resolutely empty.

"We appear to be guests of honour," Tom Wyatt says. "Shall we sit, gentlemen?" They occupy the four lesser places, and the room falls silent, almost at once. A bell tinkles, and servants appear with the first course.

The sixty guests chatter amongst themselves, leaving the four Englishmen to their own devices. The meal continues in this way for six, heavy courses, without any sign of the Doge. Then a second bell sounds, and the diners stand, and troop out into an adjoining hall. Will and the others follow suit, but are taken to one side by a strange looking youth, who is painted, and bejewelled as if he were a girl.

"Gentlemen," he lisps at them, "I am Pietro Gallo, the Doge's Private Secretary. Please, come with me. My master wishes a private audience with you." They follow the young creature down several corridors, until they have no idea where they are, finally arriving at an ornate door. The young man pauses, and arranges himself, as if he is a piece of art.

"The Doge's private quarters," the secretary tells them. "Within is the master of all that is fine and beautiful. Beware that you are not blinded by his magnificence." He knocks, and pushes the door open. Both Will and Tom go to remove their sword belts, but the young man stops them. "That will not be necessary, gentlemen," he says. "Weapons are allowed in the Doge's presence."

"Is that a good idea?" Mush asks. He was not going to give up his concealed dagger any way, but the idea of weapons so close to the head of state, strikes him as a little too trusting. The secretary simply smiles, and ushers them within. The room is furnished with rich wall hangings, exquisite furniture, and antiquities beyond price.

A tall, strongly built man rises from the desk he is working at, and beckons them to approach. Andrea Gritti looks to be in his fifties, but is now in his seventy-fifth year. He is Doge of Venice, and rules an empire that stretches from mainland Italy to Istria, and the far flung Greek islands. He also commands the greatest merchant fleet in the world, and controls the importation into the West of salt, sugar, mace, and other important spices.

"Please, come in, gentlemen," the Doge says. "I trust that Pietro has not been boring you too much, with his glowing praises of my almost God-like qualities?"

"A most interesting young fellow," Tom Wyatt says, for lack of anything else to say about so strange a person.

"He is a eunuch, of course. I purchased him from some Ottoman ruffians, who were trying to sell him as a catamite. It is my good fortune to be on good terms with the Vizier of Constantinople, so I was able to bargain hard."

"I believe it improves the voice," Wyatt replies, subduing a rogue smile.

"It does," the Doge replies. "Though I would rather lack a singing voice, than my *cozza.*"

"I agree, My Lord." Tom Wyatt places his cap over his manhood, without thinking. "Thank you for receiving us, on such short notice."

"Hardly that, Master Wyatt," the Doge says. "I have been awaiting your arrival with great interest. Ever since your master first wrote to me, a year ago."

Will Draper suppresses the urge to curse the name of Thomas Cromwell. The arduous trip to Italy was presented to him as a sudden, spur of the moment thing, giving him little time to think it over. Now he discovers that it was planned, and he is a dupe, once again. Previously he has been tricked into believing he was saving a prince, when the real task was to murder a Welsh rebel.

"Master Cromwell sends his warmest greetings," Will says, instead. The game, whatever it is, must be played out, if he is to return safely home to his new wife.

"How is the old rogue keeping?" the Doge asks. "I used to say he had… my English, it fails me …*avere una faccia da culo* ..."

"A face like his arse," Wyatt translates, and cannot help but grin. It is a compliment, meaning that Cromwell is brazen faced, and a cheeky, but likeable, rascal. "It is better left in the Italian, My Lord, but suits Master Cromwell admirably. He is in good health, and hopes that you are the same."

"I am seventy-five," the Doge replies, and shrugs. "God can call at any moment when you reach my age, my son. Did he ever tell you how he saved my life?"

"No sir," Will says. "Just that he once knew you."

"Twenty four years ago, outside Ferrara." The Doge waves them all to be seated. He is claiming the privilege of his advanced age, and wishes to tell them the story. "I was visiting the French army, as a liaison officer, between their generals, and the Senate back in Venice. We were looking to leave the alliance with the Holy Roman Empire, and join up with King Francis.

"Outside Ferrara, the French came on a mixed force of six thousand Spanish and German soldiers, and because of our vast superiority in troop numbers, we offered them battle. I was to be an observer at a great French victory. It was foolish of me, for I was not a young man, but I have had many adventures in my youth, and fancied myself a great soldier, like you, Captain Draper."

"I am hardly that, sir," Will says. "Chasing Irish rebels, and Welsh bandits is the extent of my military career."

"Still, you are more of a fighting man now, than I was at the age of fifty three," the Doge continues. "I was strutting up and down, behind three lines of French pike men, and a squadron of mounted Istrian crossbow men. To my right was a thousand Swiss mercenaries, and to my left, a regiment of English, Irish, and Welsh soldiers of fortune."

"Master Thomas once spoke of fighting for the French," Will says. "So, he was in the Italian wars?"

"Thank God, for me." The Doge opens a casket, and offers around some sugared almonds. Richard resists the urge to take a great handful. "We were about twelve thousand strong, drawn up on a low hill. The perfect position, or so we thought. Then the Franconian gunners began their devil's work, with a dozen field cannon. Their chain shot tore great holes through the French, and smashed men to pieces. Once our lines broke, there was a wild rush to save ourselves, and the Spanish came on, killing without mercy.

"I was knocked off my feet when a cannon shot landed close by, and my head was split open. I staggered around, half blind, until a kind soul pulled me onto his stolen horse, and rescued me. It was Thomas. He was a young ruffian back then, of course."

"He brought you back to Venice?"

"Yes. He saved my life, and when I asked what he wanted in return, he asked for a place with one of our banking houses. Imagine that. Not a bag of gold, or a box of jewels, but a seat at a clerks desk!" Andrea Gritti laughed at the memory. "In two years, he was the most astute young man in our Padua office, and turned his mind to the law."

"My uncle seldom speaks of his early life," Richard says. "It is as if he wishes to forget."

"Some of it, yes," the Doge replies. He offers another sugared almond. "Here, take the casket, my boy. I see you have a sweet tooth. I will have my people send more to your lodgings, tomorrow. Now, where was I? Ah, yes … Thomas left us, despite my pleas for him to stay, and returned to London. He believed he could become a great man, back home."

"And so he has," says Tom Wyatt. "Now, he seeks a favour from you, My Lord. Concerning the matter of King Henry, and his marriage. Are you familiar with the legal niceties?" The old man smiles, and nods. Of late, it is all that seems to be spoken of in Italy.

"The King, who I am told is quite a learned man, is of the opinion that the then pope … Pope Julius II, if memory serves me aright, was not authorised to grant the dispensation for his marriage to the present Queen. The difficulty arising from the fact that she, Katherine of Aragon, was his older brother's widow."

"The marriage was only allowed because of Pope Julius' intervention," Wyatt says. Will Draper and Mush are not interested in the legalities, and are ready for their beds. Richard sits quietly, absorbing the discussion, which he will repeat to is uncle, when asked, and chews his sugared almonds. "He, misguidedly, wished to help Henry, and in so doing committed a fatal error. A man may not marry his own sister-in-law. The bible forbids it."

"A difficult point, Master Wyatt," Andrea Gritti replies. "I, myself am married to a cousin. Yet the Dogessa and I live in relative harmony. What of the child, Mary?"

"The Princess be beloved by her father, even though she is much attached to the Queen. His Majesty always treats her with respect, and occasionally dines with her, as a good father should, even though she is not now of legitimate birth."

"Such a complicated life poor Henry leads," the Doge says, shaking his head. "Can he not simply take a mistress?"

"There is the delicate matter of the succession," Tom Wyatt explains. "The king has no son to inherit the throne."

"Perhaps it is God's will?"

"Perhaps it is not. Henry is a robust, and fertile man, well able to sire a dozen boys ... by the right woman. He must be free to marry again."

"Not many years ago, the French king had a troublesome wife strangled." The Doge knows there is no proof of this, but enjoys making mischief.

"It is not the English way of doing things, My Lord," Tom Wyatt replies. "The king wants it to be legal."

"And what does Thomas want?" Andrea Gritti asks. "For it is he that I owe, not your troubled king."

"Master Cromwell begs you to facilitate our progress to Rome. Then he asks that you endorse *whatever* decision the Pope makes."

"You wish me to agree with Pope Clement?" Andrea Gritti remembers how

Cromwell's mind used to work, and he smiles, for he can sense wheels within wheels. "He is a Medici, and I hate his family. If you wish, I will set myself against him, for Thomas."

"That might cause unrest between your two states, My Lord," Wyatt says. "It is enough that Pope Clement makes a decision, and that you endorse it, no matter what."

"I owe Cromwell a great favour," the Doge says. "So, I will arrange for your safe passage to Rome, and give you letters of introduction to the Holy See. Clement will grant you an audience, if only to see what you want, but he will not help you."

"I wish only a few minutes of his time."

"How can you hope to change his mind, in a few moments, when Lord Bedford failed after six months?"

"I was with His Lordship, back then, and believe he used the wrong approach." Tom Wyatt recalls having to flee for his life, with the emperor's soldiers on his heels.

"As you wish. There, that is the favour returned," the Doge tells them. "Now, we must discuss the second favour, and what I want in return."

"The two requests are but part of the one favour, sir," Wyatt says, sensing a trap of some sort.

"Not so. Cromwell saved my life. In return, I gave him an education, a bag of gold when he left, and now, an audience with Pope Clement. That is enough recompense, I think." Gritti sighed, and yawned then. "I grow tired, gentlemen. Return tomorrow, in the afternoon, and we will discuss your second request."

"As you wish, My Lord," Tom Wyatt says, motioning for Mush, Richard, and Will to stand. "We will return, tomorrow." The door opens behind them, in answer to a small hand bell which the Doge rings.

"Ah, Pietro, my sweet little *finocchio,*" the Doge says, using a slang word for homosexual. "Escort my guests back to the Piazza San Marco. Hurry, my friends, and you might yet catch the midnight mass."

"You are too kind," Richard says, tucking the box of almonds under his arm. As they are shown from the sumptuous palazzo, he turns to Thomas Wyatt. "Well, Tom, what was all that about? We seem to have collected on one favour, only to owe one back."

"I don't know," Wyatt says. "I cannot think how we might be of use to the Doge."

"Cromwell can," Will Draper tells them. "That which he wishes from Pope Clement can be obtained by a diplomat. He sends Richard to keep an eye on you, Tom, but what of Mush and I?"

"I do not see what you mean."

"No? Master Thomas could have sent any of a hundred men to guard your safety, but he chose me. Because, he has a use in mind for me."

"But what?" Tom Wyatt cannot think what his friend means.

"I am fit for nothing, except fighting, or carrying out some kind of black work." Will Draper studies Wyatt's face. "Do you know what he wants me to do, Tom?"

"On my honour, no."

"And on mine too," Richard Cromwell says. "Would anyone like a sugared almond?"

3   Traitors

"Well?" Sir Thomas More is on his knees, and has been praying for an hour. The hair shirt under his doublet prickles, and reminds him that humility is a virtue, and that his sudden flares of anger, are not. "What is it, Boscombe? You know I must not be disturbed at my devotions."

"That man is here, Sir Thomas," Wilfred Boscombe says. "The one with but a single eye, who will never give his name. He insists on seeing you, at once."

"Does he now?"

"He does, Lord Chancellor," Boscombe says, "and I am too much in fear of him to say no."

"You do well to fear him, fellow," More says, smiling to himself. "For I am all that stands between him, and Hell. Send him to my private rooms, and do not let anyone interrupt us."

The Lord Chancellor finishes his prayers, which revolve mainly around wishing ill on Cromwell and his followers, and returns to his private study. It is not as luxurious as Cromwell's, nor is the house anything like Austin Friars. More calls it Utopia, after his famous best selling book, and runs it like a monastic retreat. The food is poor, and the rewards few and far between for its servants.

"What do you have for me?" More asks, as soon as he closes the door behind himself. The one eyed man bows, and drops a sheaf of papers on Sir Thomas More's desk.

"It has taken me weeks to get to the heart of the matter," he complains. "None of Cromwell's people can be bribed. I had to buy one of Ambassador Chapuys' servants, and have him spy for me. Even then, he was able to get only the bare bones."

"Which are?" More knows that certain members of Thomas Cromwell's household have dropped out of sight, and believes them to be on some secret errand for the man. Despite employing several agents to track them, there has been no luck, until now.

"Richard Cromwell, the nephew, is supposed to be visiting his friends in Cheshire, but is not. Will Draper and his Jew friend are supposed to be in Ireland, but again, are not."

"Then where are they?" The one eyed rogue smiles, and picks up the top report. He opens the cover, and offers it to his master.

"Chapuys' man overheard Miriam Draper asking Cromwell for news of her husband, and he replied, saying that the ship had returned. I investigated, and found that the ship in question has come back from northern Spain."

"Spain?" More says. "That does not make sense. Why would Cromwell want anything to do with the Spanish?"

"He does not, sir," the man explains. "I spoke with one of the ship's officers, and he informs me, at great cost, that Draper, the younger Cromwell, the Jew, and Master Thomas Wyatt travelled on from Bilbao. Their destination appears to be Italy."

"Then Cromwell is sending his own embassy to the Pope," the Lord Chancellor mutters. He opens a drawer, and takes out a purse of silver. He counts out twenty five shillings, and drops them into the one eyed man's hand. "There, Rattary. Now, get out, and keep away, unless I call on you."

Matthew Rattary takes the silver, and leaves. He knows better than to try and ask for more. The Lord Chancellor is as parsimonious as a monk, and never spends gold, when silver will suffice. He leaves Utopia, and annoyed at his treatment, strolls down to Austin Friars. The gates are open, and the front door is attended by a small child, whose job is to direct visitors, or announce them, if need be.

"Is Cromwell home?" Rattary asks. The boy looks up, and nods his head.

"The master is at his book writin'," the child says. "Today, he is writin' in his book of devils. Get yer name

49

in that un, an' yer done for!"

"Fetch him."

"For a copper, I'll take yer to 'im." The coin changes hands, and the boy leads him into the house. He taps at one of the doors, then pushes it open, and slips his head around the door. "Gen'lemun to see yer, master."

"Who is it?" Tom Cromwell asks, annoyed at the interruption.

"A one eyed un," the boy reports. "He looks like old Hob on a bad day."

"That sounds like half of London," Thomas Cromwell mutters. "Show the fellow in."

"Matthew Rattary, at your service, Master Cromwell," the one eyed man says, and bows to the privy Councillor. "Forgive my calling without an appointment, but I have news that will be of interest to you."

"I shall be the judge of that, sir," Cromwell says. "There is the whiff of a paid man about you, Rattary. What is it?"

"The Lord Chancellor knows that you have sent men to Rome," Rattary tells him. "Perhaps I might be of use, letting you know how he will proceed."

"I doubt it," Cromwell says. "I am surprised that it has taken Sir Thomas almost six weeks to discover this. Now he knows, they are almost certainly already there. Do you think he wishes to make mischief, Master Rattary?"

"I do sir."

"Then he will use men like you, no doubt." Thomas Cromwell surrounds himself with agents, and spies, but he does not like paid informers. "The Lord Chancellor will send the law against me, having the likes of you spread tales, and fabricate evidence. If he cannot stop my embassy, he will blacken my name with the king, and try to prise me away from the Boleyn family. Am I right?"

"You are, sir."

"Then why do I need you?"

"The security at Utopia is most wanting," Rattary replies. "Why, a man might slip in, and choke the Lord Chancellor whilst he sleeps, or the entire house might catch alight."

"I see." Cromwell sighs. Politics can be a dirty business, and, when all is said and done, it is about winning. "I wonder what a man might want to do such a wicked thing? Might he wish to have a knighthood, or gold, or a well paid position?"

"The right man might want all three, Master Thomas," Rattary says. "The right fellow might only need a word."

"Do you know the Nails of

Christ?" Cromwell asks, naming a very rough tavern on the edge of Hackney. The man nods. "Go there, and await my instructions."

"Very well, sir," Matthew Rattary replies. "I am your loyal servant. Though, make me wait too long, and I must seek my wages elsewhere."

"Patience, Master Rattary," Cromwell tells him. "Here is five shillings, take a room for tonight, and tomorrow night. By then, all will be ready."

"There is nothing for you to do," the man says.

"I must be eating dinner, with friends, when the deed is done," Cromwell explains. "A good alibi will stop any gossip. Now, be off, and do as I wish."

The man bows, and slips from the house. He adds the five shillings to the fee he has from More, and goes off, whistling. If he performs his duty well, he foresees a great future.

*

"Francis!" A moment later, the small boy tumbles into the room. Cromwell is always amused by the intensity of his children, and their wish to do right by him. "I have a note, for Master Rafe. He is at Lincolns Inn Fields today, arguing in the law courts. It must be delivered, into his hand alone. Do you understand?"

"His 'and, an nonuvver," the boy says. He waits for Cromwell to finish, and shake sawdust over the still wet ink, then slips the paper into his shirt. "Am I to wait for an answer, master?"

"No. There will be no answer." The note explains that a one eyed man has offered to murder the Lord Chancellor, and burn down Utopia. It concludes by asking Rafe to ensure that Sir Thomas knows about the offer, and that the advice comes from Austin Friars.

*

That evening, Matthew Rattary is contemplating the purchase of a young whore's services, when four men burst into his room, stab him to death, and drop his body into the Thames. The next day, Sir Thomas sends a beautiful, illuminated Gospel to Austin Friars, with a short note.

Dear Cromwell,

It is good that we know the bounds, and retain a morality above the common herd. Come to dinner soon, and we will make one more attempt to settle our differences. I hope you take pleasure in this small gift, which is a token of friendship past.

Your servant,

Thom. More.

Cromwell admires the book, and is amused to find a passage underscored by More. It is Matthew 5:6

'Blessed are those who hunger, and thirst for righteousness, for they shall be satisfied.'

Cromwell recognises it as one of the Beatitudes, uttered by Christ when he gave the Sermon on the Mount. Those who have a hunger for God's righteousness will be satisfied someday, he mutters to himself. The Lord Chancellor is sending him another message, telling Cromwell that he will triumph, because he knows his service to God must come first.

For such a well read man, More is naïve. Surely, Cromwell thinks, he must understand that too great a hunger for righteousness will lead only to destruction? He picks up his quill, and writes back, thanking More, but declining the dinner invitation. Instead, he invites the Lord Chancellor to Austin Friars, where, he writes, we can discourse over richer fare than your cook provides.

It is a joke, of course, but Sir Thomas is beyond that stage, and will take it as a slight against him. These days, he thinks everything is against him. He thinks that the embassy to Rome is done, *against* him, rather than to advance the king's cause. So great a mind, yet so narrowly confined, Cromwell mutters to himself, and signs the note.

*

At midday, on the day following their first audience with the Doge, Bartolommeo Rinaldi, and five more young bucks arrive, to escort them back to the palace.

"All four of us?" Richard asks. He is desperate to tour the city, and Mush is already weary of politics. "Can not Mush and I venture out on our own?"

"I see no reason why not," Wyatt says, glancing at Will Draper. "Though you must attend, Will."

"Of course," Draper replies, reaching for his sword. "I am the bargaining chip." They go with Rinaldi, who seems to be less talkative today. Thomas Wyatt tries to draw him out, but he is not in the mood for gossip.

"Are all Venetians so moody?" Wyatt asks. "Last evening, you wished to talk all night with us."

"That was before," the young man says.

"Before what?"

"Before I understood why you

were here."

"Then you know more than us," Wyatt replies. He is short tempered with Rinaldi, and wants to know what is afoot. "I know only that the Doge is after a favour from us, but I have no idea what it is."

"My uncle is a wily old fox," Rinaldi says.

"The Doge is your uncle?" Will Draper asks.

"We are a very large family," the young man answers. "We Rinaldi's are a minor branch of the Gritti tree. Uncle Andrea uses us like his own private retinue."

"What do you think he wants?" Draper asks. "Something against our inclination?"

"Not yours, perhaps," Bartolommeo says. "Perhaps you will be only too willing to oblige."

"Pray, do not judge me, sir," Will tells the Venetian. "Rather, let me know what is on your mind."

"Seriously?" Young Rinaldi stops, and looks hard at the Englishman. "You do not know?"

"This is becoming monotonous, Tom Wyatt says. "Out with it, Bartolommeo. Out with it!"

"The Doge is locked in a power

struggle with Pope Clement," the Venetian tells them. "Rome is always looking to expand its territories, and is casting covetous eyes on Padua, the second city of the Veneto. They connive with the emperor's people to steal it from us."

"I see, and where do we fit into this?"

"That is easy. My uncle can get you close to the Pope. I think he wants you to assassinate him."

"Then he will be disappointed," Will Draper snaps. "I am not a hired murderer, my friend."

"Forgive me, but the Doge seldom fails to get his own way," Rinaldi replies. "He will find what you want, and offer it."

They stroll on to the palace in silence. Will Draper has suspected as much, but cannot believe that Thomas Cromwell would condone such a violent act against the head of the Roman church. He senses that Tom Wyatt is also surprised, and hopes the young Venetian's assessment is wrong.

*

The Doge's personal secretary is there, fluttering around them, asking if they slept well. He exhausts the list of things he can offer them, then takes them into the Doge's presence once again.

"You slept well?" Andrea Gritti asks, politely.

"Apart from the heat," Will replies. "I would not care to be here in Summer."

"Let us hope you are not," Gritti replies. "Has my little *finocchio* asked if you need anything?"

"Your hospitality is overwhelming, My Lord," Tom Wyatt tells the Doge. "We want for nothing. Now, you spoke of us doing a favour for a favour?"

"I did."

"I must warn you that my master has given me strict instructions as to our behaviour on this embassy, sir."

"Ah, someone has been upsetting you," the Doge says, shaking his head. "Not Pietro, I'm sure. So, it is my dear little Bartolommeo. What does he think I will ask of you?"

"He made no specific claims," Wyatt says, quickly. He has no wish to get the young man in trouble, especially when he might be of further use. "Though he professes nothing but admiration for you, My Lord Gritti."

"Just so. I will flog the child one day. He thinks to manipulate us into acting as he wishes. I blame Machiavelli, of course. Every young man of family believes that *The Prince* is the bible of political life. The boy wants something, so tries to make it happen by deceit, and intrigue."

"What does he want?" Will Draper asks.

"To die gloriously," the Doge says, and smiles. "Let me guess. He warns that I want the Medici Pope dead. Ah, I see from your silence that I have hit the nail on its head. Poor Bartolommeo is such a *cazzo!*" Tom Wyatt smiles at this. The word *cazzo* means 'cock' and is used to denote an idiot.

"He seeks to dissuade us from going to Rome?" Will Draper asks. "I don't understand."

"He wants you to stay with us, and help us fight." The Doge sighs at his nephews naivety. "The Pope wants Padua, but cannot move against us, as we are all allied to the Emperor Charles. In return, I cannot attack him. This is why my nephew thinks I wish you to assassinate him. I assure you, that is not the case. Were Clement to die badly, I will be the first to be suspected, and punished."

"The you must tell us what you do want," Wyatt says.

"You Englishmen are so … straight to the point," the Doge replies. "I

admire that, so will tell you straight.
Rome wishes to take Padua from me, but
cannot act directly. Instead, the Pope is
encouraging someone else to do it for
him. Do you know what a condottiero is,
my friend?"

"They are warlords, are they
not?" Tom Wyatt asks.

"Of a sort." The Doge takes them
to a huge map of Italy, hanging on his
wall. "See here. We hold the lagoon, and
the Veneto, or mainland. That includes
Verona, and Padua, our second city. If
Padua falls, then Venice will be isolated.
Here, is Perugia, in Umbria, a region
closely allied to Rome. The Lord of
Perugia is a certain Malatesta Baglioni."

Will Draper studies the map, and
nods his understanding of the situation.
Perugia is North East of Rome, and in
easy striking distance of Venice.

"You think this Baglioni fellow
has designs on you, My Lord?" he asks.
The Doge points to another part of the
map, which shows the city of Florence,
and its surrounds.

"Florence is a Medici stronghold.
Captured two years ago by the army of
the emperor, after Baglioni betrayed them
at the battle of Gavinana. He sold the city,
for gold, and the promise of Perugia."

"I see," the Englishman says.

"Rome cannot invade, but this condottiero can. What do you want from us?"

"The Senate wish to await developments," the Doge tells them. "They will sit, and wait until the Lord of Perugia has raised twenty thousand men, then call the city to arms. Too late, I say, but they will not let me act. What would you do, Master Draper?"

"Call the city to arms. Raise the peasantry, and start making pikes and crossbows. Then, march to Perugia, and burn Baglioni's little kingdom, from end to end. You have a great navy, so sail it down the coast, and land troops. Attack from the north, and from the sea, at the same time, and he will be caught between two forces, and destroyed."

"A good plan," the Doge says. "In return for my favour, Master Wyatt, I expect Master Draper to carry it out, and save Venice."

"We are but four men, sir," Tom Wyatt says. "Even for Englishmen, the odds of six thousand to one, are unfavourable."

"I am constrained, by the Senate," the Doge reiterates. "I cannot order the army to be called up, and I cannot issue invasion orders. All I can do is… remain inactive."

"I begin to see," Tom Wyatt says.

He is a diplomat, and must read where nothing is written, and understand that which has not been uttered. "Do you have a royal guard?"

"I am a democratically appointed city official, Master Wyatt, not a king, but there is the Doge's bodyguard. Two hundred Swiss mercenaries. Then there is the city's militia. About four hundred young men, who can afford a horse, and pay for their own weapons. I cannot stop the Swiss deciding to leave my service, nor can I forbid the young men of Venice to follow Captain Draper. I an helpless in the face of such iron resolve."

"Then your nephew will have his way," Will Draper says. "A rag tag army of six hundred, against tens of thousands. We will all get the chance to die with honour."

"I do not expect you to win, my friend," the Doge says. "Just disrupt the Perugian invasion, and give me enough time to rouse the Senate *cozzas* from their lethargy. My spies tell me that Baglioni is still in Umbria, raising funds, and will not move for a month or so. All of which means you have time to ride to Rome, and conduct Thomas Cromwell's business."

"And on our return?" Tom Wyatt wants the matter clearly agreed to.

"Captain Draper will conduct a

surprise attack against the Lord of Perugia. Once Baglioni responds, or crosses troops into the Veneto, the Senate will act, and I can launch our army against the Medici's tame dog. That is when it becomes an internal matter, and you Englishmen can leave. A fast galley, all the way home. You have my word on it."

"Master Cromwell says that will suffice, My Lord," Wyatt says. "For he tells me that he has never met a more honest man, nor a greater friend."

"You will make an old man cry." The Doge rings his small bell, and the castrato, Pietro tumbles in, as if he has been listening to every word. "Pietro, fetch the warrants for Master Wyatt. He is for Rome this very day. Then put yourself at the disposition of Captain Draper and his companions. Guide him, and see that his instructions are carried out, implicitly. Understood, my little one?"

"As you wish, Doge." The young man bows, and disappears.

"There, it is done." The Doge sits down, and sighs. He is seventy-five years old, and time weighs heavily on his shoulders. "I do not wish for war, Captain. I have not commanded an army for over twenty years, and I have never won a battle. Please, reassure an old man, and tell me how you will fight my little war for me."

Will Draper feels an immense sense of respect for the Doge then, and takes a seat close by. The man thinks and behaves like Thomas Cromwell, and he is sure he can work with him.

"Are all the young men as keen as Bartolommeo, sir?"

"Of course, but that is because they have never fought before," Andrea Gritti says. "They draw swords on one another, and play at duels. Some have even chased after a few bandits, but none have ever had to kill a man. My nephew will spread the word, and the young gallants will assemble when the time comes."

"No, I need them now," Will explains. "Your Swiss are trained, and know how to present arms, or stand in the face of a cavalry charge, but your young lords have no idea. I must drill them, until they obey without question."

"Master Wyatt will be gone about ten days," the Doge says. "Will that be enough time?"

"To teach them how to die, yes," Will replies, "but to win, I must have another three months, and ten thousand more men. Can you arrange that?"

"Then you would stay?"

"Find the men, and I will fight your war, for three months, but I must return home in January."

"You will do this for me?"

"For Cromwell," Will replies. "I owe him. Perhaps, by helping you, I can repay him."

"In his letters, he tells me to trust you, before any other," the Doge says. "You must be very important to him."

"He has never said so… not in words, but he treats my wife and I like his own family."

"Then, for his sake, do not take too many risks, my boy."

"I'm a soldier, sir… not a *cozza*."

"Baglioni is a dangerous man."

"I've met dangerous men before, My Lord."

"I once dined with Baglioni's uncle, who was Lord of Perugia, until two years ago." The Doge smiles at the memory. "He was a big, blustering sort of man, and I liked him, very much. He spoke of his heir, Baglioni's brother, with love, and respect. I asked him what he thought of his younger nephew. Here, this is what he said." Andrea Gritti opens a book and offers it. Will glances at what he presumes is a private diary, and shakes his head.

"My Italian is not good enough,

sir."

"Never mind, I will tell you. I wrote it down, word for word, because it amused me so much. He said: *'Malatesta Baglioni is a good for nothing, full of shit, penniless brigand, and the misbegotten son of a whore.'*"

"Not a close family then?" Will says, and cannot help but laugh out loud.

"A week later, the man was dead, under dubious circumstances." The Doge closes his diary. "The elder brother was suspected, of course, as he inherited the title, but within a month, he succumbed to a bout of mushroom poisoning."

"Dear God!"

"Indeed. Malatesta Baglioni then agreed to join forces with Florence. He betrayed the Florentines to the Pope's army, and they suffered a fatal defeat. Thus, the traitor became Lord of Perugia."

"I understand what you say, sir," Will Draper says. "I must not expect the man to behave in an honourable way, if I wish to live."

"Just so, Captain Draper. Now, would you like to inspect the palace guards? They are huge Swiss mountain men, who can swing a halberd with one hand!"

Three months. Will Draper cannot believe he has done such a rash thing, and wonders what his wife will say when he fails to get home for Christmas. Dear, sweet, Miriam, he thinks. Was there ever a more beautiful, and faithful wife?

4 A Day in Venice

Down by the waterfront, the various small waterways, leading into the heart of the great, artificial island of Venice are choked with small boats and barges. Each one is piled high with fresh fish, crabs, lobsters and small squid. So closely packed are these craft that Richard and Mush use them to cross from one side to another, without benefit of a bridge.

"Is everyone in Venice rich"

Mush asks, as the crowd are all dressed in clothes befitting courtiers, or rich merchants. He does not know that a Venetian will spend his last sou on a new outfit, even if it means he must go hungry. To the people of the lagoon, style is everything, and a finely dressed man might be a merchant, or an apprentice cobbler.

Richard is so busy drinking in the amazing sights, that he does not notice the two men stopped in front of him, examining some wares on a stall. He barges into them, and before he can apologise, one of them has pulled a knife from his belt.

"*Cozza!*" the angry fellow curses. Richard grips the man's wrist, and twists. The knife clatters to the pavement, and with contemptuous ease, the Venetian is tossed into the bay. He hits the dirty looking water with a huge splash, and the crowd roar, and applaud in spontaneous merriment.

"What is a *cozza*?" Richard asks, grabbing the second man by the shirt front. The man's knees give way, and he slumps to the floor. "Get up, you idiot. Are all you Venetians crazy?"

"Not all, sir," a swarthy man, in his middle years says, bowing low. "Permit me to present my good self to you, fine gentlemen. I am Carmino Ignazio Spinelli. You will know the name, of course, Englishman, for I am the most famous sword master in all of Italy. No ... did I say that? I mean in all of Europe, and then the world!"

"Such a modest fellow," Mush says softly to Richard. Then louder: "Signor Spinelli... why, yes. I do believe I have heard your name mentioned in the court of our king."

"Mentioned?" Spinelli considers if this is a compliment, or an insult, then shrugs. "It must suffice. England *is* a long way away. You must call me Carmino."

"So, what is a *cozza*?" Richard asks. The man at his feet goes on all fours, and tries to crawl away, unobserved. Carmino explains by grabbing his own codpiece, and giving it a symbolic squeeze. Richard growls, and kicks the escaping Venetian up the backside.

"You are newly arrived?" Carmino asks, then before they can answer, he offers his services as a guide. "The city is beautiful, but can be dangerous to those who do not understand it."

"Our thanks, Carmino," Mush replies. "We just want to see the sights."

"Then consider me at your

disposal, my young friends," he says. "Is the big one your servant?"

"My companion," Mush says. "We are here with the delegation from England, to speak with the Doge."

"So many foreigners come to Venice, these days, it is hard to keep track of them all." The Venetian sword master points over his left shoulder. "The palazzo with the white front is the Holy Roman embassy, and is full of Austrian and German spies. The building on the other side of the canal is the Spanish legation. They too are spies, but of a better class. Now, you English come to us."

"We are friendly," Richard says.

"Si? Tell the man you threw into the water!" Carmino says this with a twinkle in his eye, and they all laugh. "I am a lucky man to have found you, my friends."

"You make it sound as if you were looking for us," Mush says, suddenly quite wary. "Are you set to spy on us, or are you to be our nursemaid?"

"Neither, I hope." Carmino sees he is confusing the situation, and hurries to explain himself. "It is only that I need two friends … to act for me, in a matter concerning a lady's honour."

"Act?"

"As seconds," Carmino says.

"The Senator, Marco Duezzo has taken it into his head that I am having a... flirtation... with his new young wife, and he gave me the glove."

"He gave you a glove?" Richard is confused, and wonders what use a single glove can be to the man.

"No, he gives me the glove. He slaps my face with it, and calls me a filthy name."

"Were you having a dalliance?" Mush asks, quite intrigued by the man's indignation.

"That is beside the point," he replies. "Gentlemen should not treat one another so. Were he to seduce my wife, I would leave him to it. Though, I confess, my wife is a harridan, and I would welcome the rest. So, now I must fight with him in the Ghetto Nuovo, as soon as they let the Jews out."

"Let the Jews out?" Mush is taken by surprise. "There are Jews living in Venice?"

"Of course. Are there no Jews in England?"

"No, they were all expelled, on pain of death." Mush wishes to know more, as he is a Jew, who must hide his bloodline back home.

"How barbaric," Carmino says, obviously shocked. "Here, we make them live in the Ghetto Nuovo, and close the gates each night, until sunrise. That way, they are safe, and our church dignitaries can pretend they do not exist. It is a good idea, no?"

"How do they live?"

"Quite well, I believe. They are merchants and bankers during the daylight hours, and rank amongst the wealthiest of our people. Though, of course, we do not let them take up any sort of public office. That would be a step too far for the Pope, and he would start to make life uncomfortable for everyone."

"Then you don't hate Jews?"

"Why should I?" Carmino is now surprised. "Signor Frederico ben Joseph is my banker, and a dozen of the prettiest courtesans in Venice are Hebrew girls. They bake also the best bread, and never offer any insult to me, or to my religion. Do you hate them, my friend?"

"No, I am Jewish," Mush says. "My name is Moshe ben Mordecai. Why do you fight in the Jewish quarter?"

"No city guards to interfere," Carmino says, "and there are several fine doctors living there. This is useful for my enemies, as I am …"

"The greatest sword master in Venice," Richard says, finishing their new friend's sentence for him. "Come on, let's get off. I have never witnessed a real duel before. Will it take long?"

"A few moments," Carmino says. "My opponent is an old pupil of mine. I did my best for him, but he is slow, and has no real finesse."

*

The Ghetto Nuovo is a pentagonal 'campo' or courtyard, some two hundred paces on each, irregular side, and is walled in with an array of houses, ranging from comfortable middle class, to a couple of magnificent palazzos. One of the most magnificent of them is owned by the Anselmi banking family, and the other by the rich financier, Frederico ben Joseph, who counts both the Doge, and the Pope amongst his customers.

The two Englishmen cross one of the pair of small bridges, and go through the gate, which is closed, and locked, at each sundown hour. Any Jews found without, and any Christians found within, outside normal business hours, can receive a fine of five ducati. Many young gallants flout the regulation, and scale the vine clad walls, leaping from balcony to balcony, in search of true love. The Englishmen follow Carmino Spinelli into the bustle within.

It is reminiscent of London Bridge on a market day, with people pushing carts, selling from stalls, or baskets, and exchanging the time of day with one another. As they arrive, those chatting in the centre of the large, open space start to move to one side, and a large, circular area is formed, as if by magic. Mush has never been with some many of his own people before, and he feels a thrill of excitement.

"They expect me," Carmino says. "Word will have gone around that I am going to teach the Duezzo family a lesson. They hate the man, because he owns half of their houses, and extorts huge rents from them. My opponent will be here soon. I will present you as my seconds. Your duty is to ensure fair play, and help carry away my corpse, should I lose."

"He'll kill you?" Mush asks.

"If he can." the sword master replies. "Though I am the clear favourite to win, he has a slight chance. On the other hand, I must endeavour *not* to kill him. It would be unethical. I will wound him, a little, and honour will be satisfied."

"Best kill him," Richard says. "It will stop him coming back at you."

"If I kill him, his entire family must swear to kill me, in return, and he has six brothers, and eleven grown nephews. There is also a son by his first wife. I would be fighting duels every day of the week, for a year. No, my friend, the gentleman will settle for a quick thrust into a leg muscle, I think."

"Good day, Signor Spinelli." A thick set man, with steel grey hair arrives, with two younger men in tow. "I see you have actually managed to find two men to act for you."

"I have, Signor. May I have the honour to name ... er ..."

"Moshe ben Mordecai, and Master Richard Cromwell," Mush says, saving Carmino's blushes. "We are newcomers to your beautiful city, sir, and ..."

"A Jew?" Senator Duezzo grins, and shakes his head. "Is that the best you can manage, Spinelli - a stinking little Jew, and an ogre?" Richard looks over his shoulder, thinking some monster is behind him, then understands that they are both being insulted.

"These Senators," he growls, "buy their rank with gold don't they? Does that mean any dog can become one? Ah, I see it does!"

"Well said, Signor Cromwell," Carmino says. "These men are my seconds, sir. You belittle yourself by insulting them."

"At least the little one is in the

right place," Duezzo says.

"You dislike my race, sir?"

"Christ killers, everyone of them."

"Enough, Duezzo," Carmino says. "Let us get to it. I will draw your blood, and swear you are mistaken about me, and your poor wife, Ignacia."

"Do not concern yourself with my wife," the man says. "She is safe from all men, now."

"What have you done?" the sword master asks. He sees the glint of hatred in his opponent's eye, and fears the worst.

"I have had her head shaved, and sent her to a nunnery," Duezzo replies, smirking. "My two nephews here, held her down, whilst I flogged her. Then they had her dragged to the convent of Santa Serafina, near Verona, barefoot. I found the sight … most edifying."

"Sir, you are a dead man," Carmino tells him, and draws his sword at once. The rules of the duel are forgotten. Duezzo's nephews both draw, and it is plain that it was their intent to create this situation, so they might fall on him, together. Richard Cromwell draws his own sword, and the campo is suddenly full of the clash of steel on steel.

The action is furious, and brief.

Richard fells one of the nephews with a clumsy, overhand blow, that is powerful enough to almost sever his arm. The man screams and falls to the floor, as Mush with dagger and sword lunges and thrusts at the second nephew. The man is skilful, and evades the first rush. He ripostes, Mush side steps, and slashes his dagger down, across his attacker's right wrist.

Duezzo makes two good attempts at a lunge, parries a return thrust, and tries to duck inside Carmino's sword arm. Instead, he finds six inches of steel in his throat. He staggers back, blood hissing from the wound, and falls over in a crumpled heap. The man is dead, and both his nephews are wounded.

"His seconds need seconds," Richard declares, wiping his sword clean of blood.

"Come, the doctors will attend to them," Carmino says. "The man was a swine. I must ride to Verona, and retrieve poor, dear Ignacia."

"Can you do that?" Mush asks, wondering if he and Richard have the time to go off on an adventure.

"It is a small matter," Carmino explains. "With her husband dead, Ignacia is now the third richest widow in Venice. Once back here, she will inherit a fleet of merchant ships, and a couple of very grand palazzos. Her hair will grow back."

They cross the bridge, back into Christian Venice, and make their way to Saint Mark's basilica. There are stalls serving freshly made food, and they eat in near silence. At last the sword master speaks.

"You saved my life, my friends," he says. "Even the greatest sword master in Venice might not have managed to overcome three at once. Though I would have tried."

"He came, intending to murder you," Mush tells their new friend. "You should tell the authorities."

"Is that the English way?" Carmino smiles, and shakes his head. "No, I must reinstate Ignacia, then leave Venice, until I can raise enough blood money."

"What's that?" Richard asks.

"The family will demand my death, or an amount of gold, in return for the killing. They will want at least ten thousand ducats."

"What a strange country," Richard says, but he does understand. With successive relatives and friends all swearing revenge, if the circle of violence is not broken, the population will be halved in next to no time.

"Do you have a horse?"

"I will find one."

"Do you have money?"

"Not as such," Carmino says. "I live from lesson to lesson."

"Here." Mush takes the purse of silver, given to him by Tom Wyatt. "Enough to pay for a horse, and a few nights lodging. This Ignacia must be some amazing woman."

"Not really," Carmino says. "I was attracted by the idea of making the *cornuto* on Duezzo."

Mush shakes his head in disbelief. One man dead, and two more badly hurt, because one man wishes to make the other into a cuckold. The *cornuto*, or horns placed on the husband's head, signify that the man has an unfaithful wife.

"You let him find out?" he asks.

"I wished to humiliate him, not kill him," Carmino Spinelli explains. "His faction in the Senate do nothing for the common people. I suppose I wanted to show him up for what he was."

Mush understands. Powerful men cannot help but abuse their power. He thinks of Cromwell, Thomas More, and the king, and of how they each, in their own way, misuse their power. Perhaps, now and then, it is good for one of them to take a fall. he offers up a silent prayer that it will not be Thomas Cromwell.

"Hey, look at that!" Richard grabs his shoulder, and points out into the bay. A ship is trying to gain safe harbour, but two of the sleek war galleys appear, and cut across its bow, making it heel over.

"Is it an attack? Mush asks. Carmino Spinelli holds a hand up, above his eyes, to shade them from the glaring October sunshine.

"No, I doubt it." He stares, then nods his head in understanding. "They are flying a warning flag, but hope to make port. The authorities will not allow them to make dry land."

"Why not?" Mush asks.

"There is sickness aboard. The ship is coming from the Ottoman lands. There is wide spread *Lenticulae* around the Bosporus."

"Lentils?" Mush does not understand. "There are small lentils on board?"

"That is what they call the sickness," Carmino Spinelli says, crossing himself. "It appears from nowhere, and strikes like the Hand of God. One day, you are a robust man, then comes a sort of lassitude for two days. On the third day there is the fever, followed closely by delirium."

"It sounds like the shivering sickness, back home," Richard says, "What then?"

"About the fourth day spots appear, and they look just like lentils. Fever rages through the victim, until death claims them. In a very few cases, the stricken man, or woman, for no known reason recovers."

"It sounds horrific," Mush says, as he watches the two fighting ships herd the contaminated vessel further out into the lagoon.

"It kills within seven days," Spinelli concludes. "The doctors think it is caused by bad water, or eating rotten food. Those who have it, piss a colour akin to pomegranate wine."

The infected ship has given up the struggle to make port, and lowers its great, square sail. The harbour is lined with hundreds of people now, all staring out into the lagoon. There is a sudden puff of smoke from one of the galleys, and a flash, as they open fire with their cannon. The first ball cuts the ship's mast, and it topples sideways, into the water.

"What are they doing?" Mush cries. "They can't … it's murder!"

Another couple of cannon balls find their mark, and the ship is holed below the water line. It settles, and begins to sink, very quickly. Mush can see men on the deck, running around, and trying to leap into the water. On the galleys, trained Genoan gunners, raise muskets to their shoulders, and fire shot after shot into the desperate men. Those who do not drown, or avoid being shot, try to swim for their lives, but soldiers on the waterfront are waiting with twelve foot long pikes, to dash their brains out, before they touch land.

"Come away, Richard," Mush says, pulling at his friend. "This is no place for us, or for any decent man. Why cannot they let them land on one of the small islands in the lagoon?"

"We did," Carmino tells him. "Twenty five years ago, we let some survivors from an Ottoman ship row ashore on a tiny isle, and sent them food and water. A month later, and their plague reached us in Venice. We lost a third of our people within three months. Including my parents, and two sisters."

"I'm sorry." Mush has no answer for such a cruel twist of fate. "God only knows why these things happen."

"God?" Carmino Spinelli laughs coldly. "*Dio deve andare, e farsi fottere!*"

They walk with Spinelli to one of the small ferries that ply back and forth to the mainland, and wait with him, until it is time to depart. His early good humour is gone, and he seems shrouded in a melancholy as thick as the morning mist which often masks the lagoon.

"I hope we meet again, Carmino," Mush says. "You have enlivened an otherwise dull day."

"Oh, I doubt you have many quiet days," the sword master replies. "Not from the way you handled yourselves in the Ghetto Nuovo. You fight like professional men, Signor Moshe ben Mordecai. May I give you a word of advice?"

"I would be honoured," Mush says.

"Go back to the ghetto, and speak with your people," he tells him. "Tell them your name, and ask after relatives. Jews always have relatives. If not in Venice, then in Spain, or France. What ever you do, my friend, do not believe you are alone. Your people have a rich history. There are islands, like Cyprus and Malta, where your race mix freely with Christians and the people of Islam. Your people live openly in Jerusalem, and all across the Holy Land."

"I cannot just go," Mush says. "I have a new wife in England, and a sister too. My life is there."

"Pretending to be a Christian?"

the sword master smiles grimly. "We men are such fools. Why stay where you are not wanted? Sell up, and find your true place in this world. Failing that, come back to Venice, and we will drink, fight, and chase after other men's wives from dawn to dusk!"

"Can life be that simple?" Mush asks. He is beginning to realise that there are many different kinds of duty in the world. He is barely eighteen years old, and already has a duty to his new wife, Gwen, his friends, his sister, his faith, and … most of all, it seems, to Master Thomas Cromwell.

"Perhaps not, my friend," the sword master says, "but you are too young to spend your days watching over your shoulder for some enemy or other. Finish your business here, and try to lead a quieter life."

"Advice you do not yourself take."

"It's too late for me, boy," Carmino says with a sly smile. "Far too late!"

5 Lace Gloves, and Cheese

"God's teeth, what does the man want now?" The king is in the frost covered gardens at Whitehall Palace, walking with Lady Anne, and wants nothing more than peace and quiet. His Lord Chancellor, however, will not be set aside. "The fellow has even dragged poor Bishop Gardiner with him."

"I shall retire," Anne says, removing her hand from Henry's arm. "For this particular Thomas is not to my liking, My Lord."

"Oh, don't desert me now, my sweet," Henry moans. "Stay, and frown at them until they go away." He beckons the two men forward, and waits patiently, whilst they take it in turns to bow, and offer their best wishes. The moment the flattery ceases, he says: "Well?"

"Your Majesty, I have received

disquieting word from France, and thought it best to come to you, at once," Sir Thomas says, his face displaying something approximating a smirk.

"Though you came by Winchester, I see?" Lady Anne says, nodding at Stephen Gardiner, the recently appointed bishop.

"Bishop Gardiner is here to testify to the truth of what I must impart to you, sire."

"You think I would call you a liar?" Henry smiles, and wonders what mischief is afoot now. He thinks he is clever putting the two Thomas's against one another, but introducing Gardiner to the mix might be a step too far. "Speak, man. What is it?"

"It concerns Cromwell, sire." Sir Thomas More is preparing to enjoy his triumph. Rather than conclude Henry's annulment, he is spending his days trying to unpick everything the Privy Councillor does.

"Then should not he be present?" More's face is a picture of horror, and Lady Anne cannot help but add: "I believe he is at court today, attending to Your Majesty's business."

"Capital idea, my love," Henry says. "Send one of your girls to fetch him. There. The little Seymour wench has nothing to do."

Jane Seymour, a recent addition to the Boleyn entourage is sent off, to fetch Master Cromwell, at the king's insistence. She finds him in the long gallery, near The King's Wardrobe, where he is berating one of His Majesty's dressers.

"Stockings, sir," he is saying, as she approaches. "Please note the plural. Six pairs of the best French silk stockings have become four pairs, and one stray. Now, will you put your mind to finding them, or shall I hire someone who can count?"

The young man looks about to cry, but Cromwell pats his shoulder, offers a small, conciliatory word, and sends him about his allotted task. Jane Seymour gives a small cough from behind him.

"Do you require a doctor, Mistress Seymour?" he says, without turning around. She is surprised, and forgets to curtsey to him. Cromwell is the king's man now, and must be treated accordingly.

"How did you know it was me?" she asks.

"I have magical abilities," he says, then smiles, and points to the small window to one side. "Reflection. Though I do believe you are fond of wearing lavender oil too."

"To o much?" she asks, anxiously. Cromwell waves away her fears, and asks her what he can do for her. She has to think for a moment, then recalls her mission.

"The king wants you. He was in the rose garden, though there are no blooms … save Lady Anne, of course, but was returning to the inner chamber, with his visitors."

"There, my dear," Cromwell tells her. "You delivered the message beautifully. I shall praise you to the king for it.

"Thank you, kind sir," Jane says, and curtseys. As Cromwell makes to walk away, she stops him with a hand laid on his coat sleeve. "His Majesty is with Sir Thomas More, and another, the Bishop of … somewhere or another…"

"Winchester?"

"Yes. The Lord Chancellor seems eager to speak with the king, but Lady Anne insists you are present."

"Ah, then the man is out to make trouble." Cromwell sighs, and wonders when they stopped being friends. "Would my magic gift tell me what he has up his sleeve."

"News from France, Master Cromwell," Jane Seymour tells him. She is very slight, and rather pretty, and her voice is as light as a breeze. Ten years ago, a younger, more lustful, Cromwell would have been interested in her. Instead, he claps his hands, and calls for his man. Rafe Sadler breaks off chatting with Charles Brandon, the Duke of Suffolk, and approaches.

"Yes, sir?" he asks.

"Run to the office, and bring the red satchel, Rafe," Cromwell tells him. "I will be with the king, but you must bring it straight to me. Then, find this lady's size, and buy her two pairs of fine lace gloves."

"Yes, master," Rafe says, and bows to the girl. "I shall attend upon you presently, Mistress Jane."

Jane Seymour squeaks a thank you, smiles at this man who now seems like much less of an ogre, and hurries away. Thomas Cromwell, watches her go, and is reminded of his own daughter Jane, now eight years old, and born out of wedlock, and behind his late wife's back. The episode, with a former serving girl, shames him, and the girl is being raised by a good family in Chester, where she will want for nothing … except her father. The mother was a pretty, feather brained little thing, who did not survive the birth by more than a day or two.

The Privy Councillor shrugs off the dark memories and, forewarned, makes his way to the king's inner chamber.

*

Henry is seated on the new, pearl and gold inlaid throne, a gift from the merchants of Antwerp, and Lady Anne is standing by his side, with More and Gardiner off to one side.

"Well met, Master Cromwell," Anne says, quickly, and gives him a look that promises her support. "It seems these gentlemen wish to lay charges against you."

"No, Lady Anne, not I!" Stephen Gardiner, the recently appointed Bishop of Winchester blurts out. "I am here, merely to corroborate certain facts." Sir Thomas More throws a contemptuous glance at him, and realises that, as always, he must fight his own battles.

"Well then," Cromwell says, "we *are* well met, My Lady, and with His Majesty here to hear the truth at first hand."

"The truth of what?" Henry says, almost shouting. "Out with it Sir Thomas. You three are, after Lady Anne, my most beloved friends, and I want nothing to come between us." Cromwell has to look down, lest the king sees his smile. Henry strives to do nothing else but set them at one another.

"Then let me speak as a friend, sire … and as a concerned minister of your government," More says.

"Concerned, sir?" Thomas Cromwell interjects. "Have you laid these concerns before Parliament, and the Privy Council, as is the right and proper course?"

"I have just received the news," More replies. "My agents in France bring the most disquieting information."

"Oh no," Cromwell groans, theatrically. "Do not tell me the French king has refused my gift." The room falls into a stunned silence. The Lord Chancellor is expecting a hard fight, yet here is Cromwell admitting the truth.

"Then you admit it?" Sir Thomas asks. "You admit sending fifty thousand pounds to Paris, as a bribe to King Francis?"

"Let us call a gift a bribe then," Cromwell says, testily, "but let us also get our sums right. The figure was a hundred thousand pounds, partly in gold, and some in silver. I see where you go wrong, Sir Thomas. You ask the bishop, who has friends in the treasury, and they supplied the lower amount. Is this so, Stephen?"

"Why yes, it is," Gardiner says.

"Though I never meant any malice by the act. I simply answered Sir Thomas's query."

"As you should, My Lord Bishop," Cromwell replies. Then he folds his hands across his stomach, and lapses into silence.

"Well?" the king asks. Cromwell appears surprised by the king's statement and spreads his hands wide.

"Sire?" he says. "I am waiting for Sir Thomas to lay his charges, and did not yet see anything to respond to."

"Fifty thousand pounds, sir!" More says.

"One hundred thousand," Cromwell says. "Now, why do you say this is a bribe?"

"It would seem so. Why else would you send … a hundred thousand pounds to the enemy of our king?"

"Go steady, Lord Chancellor," Thomas Cromwell says. "For the king is at peace with France these past four years, and loves *François* like a brother."

"That is so," Henry says, "though I do not love him a hundred thousand pounds worth, Thomas."

"Fifty thousand, sire," Cromwell replies, then turns to Lady Anne. "Mistress, your indulgence, if I may ask you something?" Anne smiles, and nods consent. "Has not the king put into my hands, the handling of his annulment?"

"He has, Master Cromwell. He told me so, himself, and swore you would achieve my desires for me, within two years."

"And I was to have a free hand, unencumbered by the Lord Chancellor, or even the Privy Council?"

"What?" This is news to More, and he can feel his face turning red. "A free hand, surely not, sire?" Henry nods. He has done it to placate Anne, and cannot go back on his word without looking dishonest. More shakes his head in disbelief. "But this does not explain why fifty thousand..."

"A hundred thousand."

"A hundred then, damn it!" More loses his temper for a split second, then takes a deep breath. "The fact remains, you send money gifts to Francis. The man does not support the king in the matter of the annulment, and will never change his mind. Your bribe must be for an altogether different thing."

It is then that Rafe Sadler comes in, and goes straight to Cromwell. He bows to the room, and hands him the papers he was sent to fetch. The lawyer thanks him, and rummages through the documents, placing them in order. He hands the top sheet to the king.

"A letter, from me, to Francis, asking what his plans are for one of his many illegitimate daughters. I believe her name is Marie, after the scullery maid who bore her for the king."

"I hear that our dear cousin, *François*. has more than a dozen bastards," Anne says, slipping into the slight French accent she adopts when wishing to impart something a trifle naughty. She often talks to Henry in this voice, and it drives him mad with unrequited passion.

"I am only interested in Marie, Lady Anne," Thomas Cromwell says. He hands over a second sheet. "Here is the reply, from his Prime Minister, asking me what my interest is in the child. I respond … here… saying that I have a marriage in mind, for which I am willing to pay fifty thousand English pounds."

"Marriage?" Henry is astonished. He has a bastard son, Harry Fitzroy, who needs a bride, but he is promised now to Norfolk's girl. "I cannot barter with Fitzroy, Thomas. You go too far!"

"No, sire, not your most excellent son," Cromwell explains. "I sought out an altogether different kind of union for the girl. In this letter, you will see that *François* drives a hard bargain, once he sees what I am up to. He demands a hundred thousand."

"But you only sequestered fifty," Stephen Gardiner says.

"Correct. I raised the balance personally, from my own resources."

"You can lay hands on fifty thousand pounds?" Henry is even more surprised at the admission.

"In a manner of speaking," Cromwell replies. "I intend sending the fifty thousand, along with the fifty from the treasury to Paris during the next few weeks. I only await word that the groom is willing."

"Who is the lucky fellow?" Lady Anne asks, enjoying the clash immensely.

"Alessandro de Medici, My Lady."

"Who may that be?" More demands, but the king knows the man, and roars with laughter.

"No, I cannot believe it. Not even of a rogue such as you, Thomas!" Henry roars, and wipes his eyes free of laughter tears.

"Should I know the gentleman?" Anne asks, puzzled.

"The Pope's bastard!" Henry declares. "Wonderful. Why it is almost worth a hundred thousand, just to see his face."

"I wager the Bishop of Rome will be pleased, sire." Cromwell says, with a beaming smile on his face.

"You come with half a tale, gentlemen," Henry says. "You may leave us. I have much to talk about with my *chief* councillor."

The moment More and Gardiner leave, Henry turns to Anne, and squeezes her tiny hand.

"The fellow will not let me make him an earl, my sweet," he says. "How can I reward him?"

"I still don't understand," Anne says, but is waved into silence.

"The money disquiets me, Thomas," he says to Cromwell. "I see about the treasury money, but where, in God's name did you find your share? I do not pay you above five hundred a year."

"I had some savings, and sold a few properties, sire, which raised ten thousand. The rest, I took from Norfolk and Suffolk. Twenty thousand each."

"They do not have that kind of cash," Henry replies, warily.

"No, sire. I arranged for them to borrow the sums from some Venetian bankers I know.

"On what surety?"

"On yours sire."

"Mine? Dear God, Cromwell,

what are you thinking of?"

"Your Majesty guarantees the loans, and both of the dukes pledge their estates to the crown, if they default. It will tie them to you, sire. When they default, we buy the debt up, and they are your vassals. For the next hundred years, they will be buying back their own property."

"And if they disagreed?"

"I would have told them you were displeased with them, and thinking of sequestering their lands. Under the new laws, refusing the king, is treason."

"You clever fellow," Henry says. "I would not do that to them."

"Of course not, sire, but we do not need to tell them that, do we?"

"Is it honest?"

"You have said nothing," Cromwell replies. "It is only my honour that is tarnished."

"Will it work?" Henry asks.

"It will, sire. Francis is strapped for money, after his latest disastrous war. The man is no soldier. Perhaps if Your Majesty were to visit his army, and offer to lead the next charge?"

"By God, yes. Did I ever tell you how I swept the field clean with one charge?" The king has moved on, and Cromwell's plans can advance, uninterrupted.

*

"The man must be in league with Satan," Stephen Gardiner, Bishop of Winchester says, then retracts at once. "No, do not think it. Charge Cromwell with witchcraft, and it is you and I who will end up on the fire. You did not plan well enough."

"You were a great help, Master Bishop," Sir Thomas curses. "Why did you not support me?"

"I support no one, except the king," Gardiner replies, rather sanctimoniously.

"And God?"

"That goes without saying."

"Yet you do not do your best for Rome," More says. "You would have heretics running the church."

"Tell me, Sir Thomas, if God hates the protestants so much, why does he allow Martin Luther and the rest to flourish all over the continent? Perhaps he does not care for Rome anymore. The place is venal and corrupt."

"Yes, and Cromwell's mission is there by now." More is fuming with anger. "They will see the Pope."

"To what end?" Gardiner replies. "Were they to give this hundred thousand to Clement, he would laugh at them. It is not enough to buy two cardinals, and that is how many you must bribe to see him."

"They will try to push the annulment through. If they succeed, Henry will have no faith in us any more."

"They may push all they wish, for Pope Clement will never change his mind. He will sit on his decision, until the halls of hell freeze over, and Henry is too old to care."

"Yes, you are right," the Lord Chancellor says. "Forgive me, old friend, for being so rude to you. I am sure you will do your best, as your ecclesiastical conscience allows. How is it, being a bishop?"

"Hard, sir, very hard," Gardiner says, thinking of the two mistresses - the most wanton pair of sisters - that he has been forced to abandon. "My monks watch me like a hawk, and never cease from telling me what my holy duty is. I am a prisoner, sir… a prisoner!"

*

"I seek Mistress Miriam Draper, girl." The tall, dark haired man says. "Pray, fetch her, please, and there is a penny for your trouble."

"It is no trouble, sir, but keep your coin. I am Mistress Draper." Miriam looks the man up and down, and sees that, apart from having curlier hair, he is very much like her absent husband.

"A thousand apologies, mistress, I expected an older lady."

"Then I am sorry to disappoint you," Miriam replies, smiling at this handsome reminder of Will. "Do you have a name, sir? The accent tells me you are from the north."

"I am from the city of Chester, Mistress Draper, and my name is Edward Small. I am, for my sins, a merchant."

"Come in, Master Small," Miriam says. She calls for refreshments to be brought, and takes the man into the best withdrawing room. It contains the most comfortable seats, the best wall hangings, and a small table, with her chess board and pieces, set up on it. "What can I do for a fellow trader?"

"You come to the point well, Mistress Draper. I have come to London in the hope of furthering my family's business."

"Please, call me Miriam… and I shall call you Edward."

"My friends call me Ned, Miriam. I hope that you will too." He cannot help but smile at the girl. She is a rare beauty, and he has a heart, like any other man.

"Very well, Ned. To business. How did you come upon me?"

"It was not hard," Ned Small

replies. "I wish to sell my wares in London, so visited all the markets I could find. At each one, there was mention of Miriam Draper, and her market stalls. So, I sought you out, thinking to find a clever lady, much like my mother. Imagine my surprise when I find a goddess of wit and beauty."

"A *married* goddess," Miriam says, and blushes at the thought that he needs to be told. "My husband is away … in Italy. With my brother… to see … the Pope."

"And he leaves you here, alone?"

"I have Master Cromwell," Miriam says, feeling foolish. "He is like a guardian angel."

"Thomas Cromwell?" Ned Small's demeanour changes. He is suddenly on his guard. "The king's man?"

"The same. He is a good man."

"Then we must speak of different men. I hear he is not a man to cross, and can be a dangerous enemy."

"But a good friend," Miriam replies. "Are we going to talk business, or not, sir?"

"I have offended you," he says. "I should not listen to idle street gossip."

"No, Ned, I am not offended," Miriam tells him, "but Master Cromwell is slandered mercilessly by the Lord

Chancellor, and high church men."

"You move in very heady circles," Ned Small says. "Let us begin again. Hello, my name is Ned Small, and my family make cheese. Cheshire cheese is smooth, and rich flavoured, and not readily available in London. There, that is what I needed to say, from the first."

"I sell goat's cheese," Miriam says. "How many rounds can you supply?"

"I am prepared to open a warehouse nearby, and hold three months worth at a time, that you may draw from, as required."

"Will your cheese last?" Miriam asks. "The stuff I sell, turns inside a couple of weeks."

"We wrap them in cloth, and wax them, tight shut," Ned explains. "They will keep for two, or even three years, without drying out."

"I see, and what of my end of the bargain?"

"You must undertake to sell my cheeses on your stalls, and pay me within a month."

"I will pay, cash on the nail, Ned," Miriam says, " if you give me a keener price."

"I will reduce my price by a shilling a round for cash, providing your people collect. They are weighty, and you will need a carter."

"And what profit will I make?"

"Sold by the wedge, you will make six, or seven shillings a round," Ned says, persuasively. "Say you sell a cheese a week on your stalls ... which number a dozen, I believe ... then you will profit by three pounds twelve shillings, less cartage costs."

"I have fifteen stalls now," Miriam says. She closes her eyes, and calculates. "That comes to two hundred and thirty pounds, for we do not trade on holy days. When can we start?"

"We can be ready within the month." Ned holds out his hand, and they shake. Miriam feels the warmth travel up her arm, and into her cheeks, making them blush under the olive skin. "Now we have shaken on it."

"Good... you can let go of my hand now, Ned."

"My apologies," he says, looking into her eyes, and finally, releasing her hand. "Shall we have a lawyer draw up a legal document?"

"Why?" Miriam says. "Either we trust each other , or we do not." She thinks how the venture will improve her profits two fold, and of how pleased her husband will be. "What else do you do,

103

Ned?"

"The family make cheese," he says, "but I have friends who make various things that you might sell."

"Then we can increase our business even more," Miriam says to him. "If you bring the produce south, I will open more stalls, and accommodate each supplier... through you. In that way, we each make a profit."

"That sounds a goodly plan. We must discuss it at length."

"Of course. You must come to dinner, tonight." The words are out, before she can think properly, betraying her interest in him. He smiles, and agrees.

"I dare say you set a better table than the tavern I am staying in," Ned says. "I will bring a sample of my cheese. Shall I bring some wine too?"

"I want for nothing," Miriam replies. "Might we say, eight o'clock?"

"That will be ... quite splendid," he says, then notices the board. "Oh, your husband is a chess player?"

"It is mine, sir," Miriam replies, tartly. "My poor brain can just about master the moves."

"Then let me teach you, after dinner," Ned says, happily. "For I have never been bested yet!"

Miriam escorts him out, and

sends one of the small boys who loiter, to take him safely back to his lodgings. It is only when he is gone that she realises the enormity of what she has done. Then she pulls herself up, sharply. Where is the sin, she thinks? It is, after all is said and done, just dinner, with a future business partner. So, what if her husband has been gone seven weeks, and what if Ned Small is almost as handsome as Will?

"God have mercy," she says to the fast flowing Thames, "what is wrong with me?"

"Yes, mistress?" Young Jonah Scully, a new waif, who has taken to hanging about the place, is squatting by the river's edge, hoping for a bowl of soup, or a coin to run an errand. "Do you have need of me?"

Like half of Stepney, he has heard about the benevolent Cromwell clan, and their generosity to the poor. His friend, who tends the horses at Austin Friary, tells him that the new house, run by Mistress Miriam Draper is of the same mind, and will always find a use for a willing lad.

"Boy, do you know where Austin Friars is?"

"Me and half of England, lady," he replies, getting quickly to his feet. "It's back from the river, near where the old monks live."

"Good. You must run there, and ask to speak with Master Cromwell. If anyone tries to turn you away, tell them that Mistress Draper sends you. Understood?"

"I'm poor, lady, not a natural fool."

"Here is a penny. Tell the master you come with an invitation to dinner. If he can't come tonight, at eight, you are to go on to the Chapuys house, next door, and beg the ambassador to come."

"Shall I ask both, if the first 'un agrees?"

"Yes, do that."

"And what then if they both say no?" the boy asks, sharply. "Am I to keep a knockin' 'til some bugger says yes?"

"Yes, even if it's Old Hob from Hell," Miriam tells him, and shoos him on his way. Scully smiles to himself, and sets off at a steady trot. He has a penny in his pocket, and will almost certainly be offered something for his trouble by the Austin Friars lot. Things, since he ran away from home, are looking up.

*

"At eight, you say?" Thomas Cromwell is perplexed. He does not know the lad, and is surprised at so peremptory an invitation from Miriam Draper.

"Anything else?"

"Only that I am to go on to the Spanisher's place, and ask him too. The lady is fair desperate for company, an' no mistake, guv'nor!"

"Don't be cheeky, boy," Cromwell snaps, but relents at once. He can recall his own impoverished youth, and knows the boy is only trying to make his way. "Here, a shilling for you, child. Use it wisely, and it might save you from the gallows." The boy is overcome at so lavish a gift, and goes down on one knee.

"I thank you, sir. Master Cromwell is known for his loving kindness to us waifs an' strays. Can I speak, wiv' out you beating me?" Cromwell cannot help but smile at the lad's behaviour, and beckons him to rise.

"What do they call you?"

"Scully, sir."

"I knew a Branwell Scully once."

"My father, sir. A bully, and a bastard, if ever there is one."

"Does he still go about hooking?" The art of hooking, or lifting goods from open windows, and doorways with a shepherd's crook is rife amongst houses in the better neighbourhoods, and is punishable, like most things, by hanging. "I knew him, as lads together, and yes, he is as you claim him to be."

"He runs a couple of bawdy rooms, over in Putney, and won't miss me, sir."

"Do you sleep at the Draper house?"

"Nah, I kip out under God's tiles, Master Cromwell."

"Then you shall sleep in my stables tonight. Now, what would you tell me, child?"

"The girl ... Mistress Draper," the boy says. "I was sitting out by her door, and hears this sharp looking coxcomb talking to her, as though she were some buxom maid, instead of one as has made her vows. For once a young woman promises to '*be bonaire, in bed and board*' to a man, she should be left, unassailed."

Cromwell understands the boys reference to the part of the marriage vow that binds a woman to chastity, save with her true husband, and realises that Miriam is sending him an unspoken message.

"Master Scully, go to the back door, and ask for Rafe Sadler," the Privy Councillor tells the boy. "Tell him that you are to be suited out in my livery, and put to work as a court runner. A shilling a week, a bed, and regular meals. What say you?"

"What says I?" Scully cannot

believe his luck. "I'm your man, sir …
from dawn to cock-shut!"

6 The Field of Mars

Will Draper is aching from head
to toe, and wonders when he started to
become so unfit. He has been drilling, and
training his Swiss giants all day, trying to
make them into a real fighting company,
rather than a splendid spectacle on the
parade ground. He wishes to teach them
how to swing, in formation, without
breaking ranks, and is being helped by
Richard who has insisted on helping.

The manoeuvres are designed to
turn the Swiss into a huge battering ram in
battle, but it is hard to be dainty with
twelve foot halberds. It is not until the
heat of the afternoon is at his worst, that
Richard comes up with a sensible idea.

"Why must they be twelve feet
long?" he asks, after much pondering.
"Cannot they manage with six feet, or
eight?" The answer, of course is, yes, they
can shorten the staffs. It means the

horsemen might be able to get a couple of feet closer, but Will does not think that is a problem. The shafts are shortened, and by the evening, the Swiss are handling them like experts, and can do a *volte-face*, or execute a pivot turn on command. Richard feels it is a personal triumph, and swaggers about like a newly promoted General.

"Your men seem to like my friend," Will asks one of the Swiss sergeants. The man, a big, broken nosed creature with twenty years service under his belt nods, sagely.

"He is like us," the man admits. "*Rickhard Krummel* is a giant, and loves to fight. Put him over us, and we will charge Satan for him!"

"Then it is so," Will Draper decides. "*Krummel* shall be your officer, from now onwards."

*

Mush is with the young bucks, who flock to join the rag tag army that is to fight under no-one's banner, except their own. Word travels fast, and by lunchtime there are almost three hundred and twenty mounted men, keen to do battle. The young Englishman splits them into two companies, and has them each choose a captain, and two lieutenants.

They are all armed with swords

and daggers, and some have a small, circular shield, no bigger than a dinner plate, strapped onto their left forearms. Although the Swiss are armed with breastplates, and steel *Cabasset* helmets, the gentlemen scorn them, and wear feathered caps, and woollen doublets. Mush sees one man with a strange contraption hanging from the pommel of his saddle, and calls him over, eager to see this latest design in firearms.

"My father bought it for me," the young man boasts. "The longer barrel makes my musket more accurate. I have brought down birds in flight, whilst out hunting in the marshes."

"They are not like the usual arquebus," Mush says, examining the strange, narrow barrel of the gun. "Can I see how you load it up?"

"Surely, signor," the young man says, proud to be singled out to give a demonstration. He produces an array of wadding, lead shot, and black powder in a small flask, and goes through the motions at a laboriously slow pace. At last, he draws back the heavy hammer, and raising the gun to his shoulder, discharges it into the warm air. The flash, and resultant crack of sound makes both men and horses turn about in consternation.

"One ball of lead?" Mush asks.

"Is that effective?"

"It is quite enough to bring down a large animal, signor," the young buck replies, with smug good humour.

"Have you ever shot at a man?" says Mush.

"No, of course not, sir," the young man admits.

"Then we must teach you how to kill, properly," Mush tells him.

"We are at your command, Signor Mush," he replies.

"Who else has these muskets?" Mush asks, and is pleased to find a dozen more have them, and another twenty have the more cumbersome arquebus. He details them off to join Will's group, and also sends another six who have powerful hunting crossbows, and profess to be wonderful marksmen.

The young Jew is beginning to understand that all Venetian men consider themselves perfect at most things. He admires their arrogance, but hopes it does not get them killed, one day.

"Do you all have powder and shot?" Will asks, and finds that they are well provided for. It seems, Bartolommeo tells him, that an unknown benefactor has bought them a butt full of the newest, course ground gunpowder, and donated fifty horses to those young men too impoverished to own their own.

Will smiles, recognising the benevolent hand of the Doge, and explains why those with guns are now with him. Mush has recognised their worth, and wasted no time in letting his comrade know.

"Our Swiss pike men are a most formidable force," he tells them, "but they are a defensive, rather than an offensive, company. With you armed men, we are now a pike and shot regiment. It is a tried and tested way of fighting, and, with God's help, we will win out."

*

For the next two days, Will drills his men, teaching them this new method of warfare, and tries to instil into them the belief that they can overcome the infamous condottiero and his mercenary army. Mush grins at his mixture of English, Italian and French phrases, as he forges the men into a better, more cohesive company.

"I doubt I can fight like that," Bartolommeo observes, watching the close drilled square, with its heart of musketry.

"You won't have to," Mush tells him. "You gentlemen are our light cavalry. I will teach you how to keep your horses abreast in the charge, and how to hold your swords."

"I have no problem with my blade," one of the men says, executing a quick left and right cut. "My sword master counts me amongst his very best pupils, Signor."

"Can you do that on horseback, good sir?" Mush is grateful for a chance to demonstrate, rather than have to drill them all individually. "Do you know how to charge a man down?"

"Surely, they always run from a man on horseback," the young man says, likening warfare to fox hunting.

"Hush, Paolo," says Bartolommeo Rinaldi, but Mush waves him into silence.

"Come, Signor Paolo," he says, goading. "Mount up, and ride me down. I wager you one of your ducats that I am the better man."

"You will run, and have me chase you all over the training field." Paolo suspects some sort of a trick. "I have no wish to play the fool, sir."

"If I step back, or aside, you win," Mush tells him. "Come now, all your friends are watching. What will they say about you to the ladies. Oh, little Paolo was afraid to fight a man on foot!"

Paolo curses, springs into the saddle, and crouches over, sword pointed ahead. He kicks the horse into a gallop, and surges forward at the young Hebrew. Afterwards, opinion will be divided as to what actually happens, as it was so quickly over as to deceive the naked eye.

As the rider approaches, Mush goes down onto one knee, draws his dagger, and dips his head under the point of the man's blade. At the same time, he slashes through the saddle's cinch. Paolo looks foolish, as he misses his quarry, then even more so as his saddle slips to one side, and tumbles him to the ground.

The young Venetian is winded, and angry. He grips his sword, intent on running Mush through. Before he can rise, the lithe Englishman is on him, tapping his chest with the tip of his knife.

"Master Paolo, I think you are dead," he says, and the others burst into applause. Mush offers his hand, and helps to pull the young man to his feet. He slaps him on the back, and puts away his dagger. "Listen to me, Paolo, and I will teach you how to charge, and when not to. I will show you how to turn an opposing horseman, and kill him. Yes, gentlemen, kill him. That is why you are all here."

"Well said, Master Mush," Bartolommeo says. "Kill or be killed, eh? I hear this condottiero, Baglioni, is a wolf."

"Really? Well, my friend, wolves can be skinned, can they not?" Mush knows that a man's reputation can be a powerful weapon, and wishes to deflate his enemy. "I hear that he uses poison, rather than a sword, and treachery, rather than a crossbow. A man such as that has no honour left, and should not be feared in battle. All I can tell you is, face him without fear, but do not eat mushrooms with him!"

They all laugh, and the process of bonding together, almost as brothers, is underway. Mush will turn them into competent soldiers, but he cannot make them kill. That is something that must come from inside yourself. He keeps them working, regaling them with tales of violence, until they stop thinking that it is all an adventure.

"How did you feel, after you killed your first man, Signor?" one of the more timid of them asks. Mush frowns, and tries to recall his emotions. He was fourteen, and a footpad had sprung out on his family, on the Norwich road. Without thinking, the young Hebrew had drawn, and thrown his knife, meaning only to scare the man away. Instead, he had scored a hit, and the man was down on the ground, spewing blood from his throat, and mouth.

"Good," Mush admits. "I felt relieved to still be alive, and happy to have destroyed my enemy. There is no room for sentiment in the heat of battle. A few months ago, I was in Wales, fighting, and a friend made a mistake. He wounded his man, and then spared his life. The rogue turned, and struck down another of our company. It is not only your own life that you must look to, gentlemen. Guard the man to your left, and hope the man to your right does the same for you."

"There speaks a Cromwell man! Are you, by any chance, Thomas Wyatt, sir?" Mush turns at the sound of another English voice, and finds a stocky man in his thirties, and carrying a heavy jute sack over his shoulder. *"So, does Vulcan come down to the Field of Mars, with hammer and anvil in his arms!"*

"I beg your pardon?" Mush asks.

"Ah, then you are not the poet, young sir. Thomas did not give any great description. He is a man of few words, and sparing with his ink."

"Do you know Master Cromwell, sir?" Mush asks, warily.

"May I name myself, young fellow," the man says, dropping the sack, "as Edward Wotton, zoologist to the Doge of Venice. I am to be your farrier, and ostler during the coming expedition. See here, I have a sack of horseshoes, to start us off."

"Then you are welcome," Will Draper says, coming over to them, "but my comrade asked how you know Master Cromwell."

"We write to one another," Wotton says, in an off hand manner. "He is interested in butterflies, and other such fauna. I tell him what I can."

"About insects? I am sure my master is grateful," Will says. Another Cromwell agent, he thinks. How many does he have, the world over? "When next you write, please tell him how you find us, sir. That is to say, we are well, and our enterprise is going well."

"He will be pleased to hear of it," Edward Wotton replies. "Now, where do you want these shoes?"

"Richard Cromwell is our quartermaster," Mush says.

"Is that scurrilous dog here?" Wotton asks.

"He is, you rogue!" Richard shouts, and the two men rush at one another. Just as it seems they will clash, they embrace, and Richard hoists the older man from his feet.

"Still a great ox," the zoologist cries. "I swear, gentlemen, he was the worst pupil I ever taught!"

"Then he has not changed at all," Mush says.

"It seems our numbers swell, daily." Will can always use another man.

"Wait until tomorrow," Wotton says, tapping his nose. "I have information that there are two English ships due in on the next tide, with crews ready to earn some gold. I can promise you another fifty hard fighting Englishmen for the task ahead."

"Then let us pray they do not carry any sickness," Mush says. "For the Venetian cure is harsh indeed."

"Ah, you saw that," Wotton says. "Most unfortunate, but necessary. Once ashore the *lentulae* can wipe out whole families, in days. We can fight a dozen condottieri, good sir, but we will always lose out to the lentils!"

*

"I believe you have something to tell me, Signor," Malatesta Baglioni says. The man, a short, ageing merchantman is sobbing in pain, as he hangs by his wrists from a convenient roof beam. The condottiero puts a hand under his chin, raises his head, and stares into his eyes. "No? That is a great pity, Signor Micheletto. My man led me to believe that you want to tell me all about the Venetian plans laid against me."

"My... Lord... I know nothing," Gian Micheletto gasps, as his own body weight almost tears his arms out of their sockets. He locks his gaze on Malatesta Baglioni. "I am but a poor merchant, on my way to Genoa. I beg you to have mercy on me."

"Liar!" Baglioni slaps the man twice, hard, across his tear stained face. "You are the Doge's agent in Umbria. You are familiar with the workings of the Venetian navy, and know what their intended movements are. You will tell me their strength, and the numbers of their forces. How will they defend themselves? Do they know I am coming? I can't hear you, Gian. Speak up. Last chance." There is only silence. Baglioni raises his gloved hand, and smashes it into the man's face over and over. Then, he crosses to the door, and calls to one of his men.

Gian Micheletto is almost at the end of his tether, but will not betray his master, no matter what. He stares through bruised, and blood glazed eyes, as his wife, son, and daughter are dragged into the room. Malatesta Baglioni pulls his head up, and nods to his man. The soldier draws a knife.

"Which one first, My Lord?" the man asks, in a matter of fact way. The condottiero ponders, then sees the hatred in the eyes of the young girl, and turns to the mother. Her dress is torn, and her face is bruised. It looks as if some of his men have been sporting with her whilst they were waiting for him to begin.

"The woman, I think." Malatesta Baglioni says. "Was she satisfactory?"

"After a few slaps, sir," the man replies. "She quieted down when we offered to drag the girl in too."

"Such a noble sacrifice," Baglioni says. "Proceed."

The captain of his bodyguard nods, and cuts the misused wife's throat, with one swift slash. He holds her up for a moment, as the blood gushes then, casually, tosses the body to one side. Gian Micheletto cries out in horror.

"How many of you had her?"

"About a dozen," the captain replies. "There were plenty of takers, once I'd broken her in."

"A dozen men, Micheletto," the condottiero muses. "And she took them, as docile as a pet bird. One after the other. Why, I might even suspect she enjoyed it. Tell me your secrets, my friend."

"May God curse you," the man groans. "May you not see another Christmas tide."

"Oh dear, and I so love the festivities," Baglioni tells the suspended man. "Now the boy."

"No!"

"Then speak."

"You are a traitor, and a coward," Micheletto spits. Baglioni nods, and the captain pulls the boy's head back. He twists away, and tries to bite the man. The big soldier curses, and punches the boy to the floor, where he stabs him in the heart. The child's blood runs across the earthen floor, towards the condottiero's boot.

"Only one of your little family left, now" the condottiero says, harshly. He crosses the room, and pulls the girl's head up. Her large, dark brown eyes are blazing with hatred at him. He removes a glove, slips his hand into the top of her dress, and cups one of her small breasts. "A remarkably pretty girl, Gian. How old are you, my sweet little one… fourteen … fifteen? The girl cannot speak. She is rigid with horror, as his hand explores her young body. "Still a virgin, Gian?"

The hanging man remains silent. Malatesta Baglioni removes his intrusive hand, and signals to his man, who pulls the girl over to the low wooden table by the window. He thrusts her, face down, across it, and hoists up her skirts. The condottiero admires the exposed legs and rear for a moment, then begins to unfasten his thick leather belt.

"Please… God… please." The suspended man is sobbing.

"Never mind wailing to God, you stupid fool," the condottiero snaps. "You *know* I am going to kill you. First though, I will pleasure your daughter, as you watch. Then my men can troop in, and have their share too. You can stop it. Tell me what I want to know, and I swear to spare her."

"On your honour?"

"On the Holy Bible," Baglioni says, placing a hand over his heart. "You must die, but she will live on, her virtue intact. You have my word. Now, speak!"

"There are over fifty Venetian war galleys hidden along the coast," Gian Micheletto says. " Before the month is out, they will be filled with troops, and sail down the coast. Three thousand men will land at Rimini, and then ravage the coastline. When you move against them, the Doge's main force will cut across country, into northern Umbria, and turn south. They will force march behind you, and storm the city of Rome. Twenty thousand men, and cannon. Your forces will be split in two, traitor."

"You lie!"

"Pope Clement is a coward. Rome will sue for peace, rather than be sacked again." Gian gasps out. It is hard

123

to speak through the pain. "Then we will turn about, and catch you between our two armies. You will crack like a walnut under our boots."

Malatesta Baglioni draws his dagger, and drives it into the man's chest. He groans, and sags forward, his last thought being of how he has told the great lie. If the condottiero falls for it, he must split his army, and weaken his position. It is a small thing, but all the dying man can do for his beloved Venice.

"God piss on Andrea Gritti," the condottiero curses. "Where, in Satan's name did he get together over twenty thousand men from?"

"Mercenaries," his captain guesses. "He has some Swiss pike men. Big, hard bastards they are. Perhaps he has bought some more. Then there are always the Milanese. They will fight for anyone with enough gold to pay them. The weasel faced *cozza*."

"Twenty thousand men on land, and fifty galleys full of more fighting men." Baglioni is pensive. It means he will be fighting an equal sized force, but on two fronts. "The galleys will have to move before November, or risk the bad storms. They will land at Rimini, and march down the coast, then inland to Perugia."

"Only two or three thousand, My Lord."

"There are several ways they can come. It will take a third of my men to block their advance," Baglioni says. He is a master tactician, and is already seeing events in his mind's eye. "Then Gritti will thrust out, and down on Siena. Once the town falls, he will move on towards Rome. I doubt I will have enough men left to defeat him."

"The emperor will not let the Doge do that," his captain says. "He will order him to desist."

"It will take a month for the Emperor Charles to act. By which time, Perugia is under siege, and Venice will have Siena, and half of the Umbrian countryside in its hands." Baglioni bangs a fist into his open palm. "Order Baldini to take a thousand men, and ride to Rimini. Secure the port, and stop the Venetians landing. I will keep my Sicilian company, and two hundred horse here, in Perugia, to guard the town against a citizens uprising. The Doge might try to buy the town's folk."

"Yes, sir. What about their main force?"

"They will expect us to try and cut the road to Rome, but we will not. Our main army will swing, in a great arc, around the Doge's army. Once behind him, he is cut off from the Veneto. We will storm the city, and sack it, whilst he watches helplessly."

"Surely, he will fight," his man says.

"Let him. We will be on ground of our own choosing, and we will have cannon. The Lombard's have cannon for hire. We will pay for them, and cut Andrea Gritti's army to pieces. See to it Valdo."

"Yes, sir," Valdo replies. Then he realises he is still gripping the young girl by the neck. "What about this little bird?"

Baglioni considers. His mistress is visiting her mother in Florence, and is becoming quite tiresome, of late. Perhaps a fresh, young lover might enervate him for the struggles to come.

"What is your name, girl?"

"Pippa," the girl says, as Valdo allows her to rise, and rearrange her dress. She looks him in the eyes, despite shaking with fear, and horror.

"She is rather pretty, for a commoner. Send her to my quarters, for later" he says.

"What about your promise?" the captain says. He is a superstitious man, and fears the breaking of oaths. "You swore to spare her, on the holy bible."

"And so I will, for the next few days. Then, if she does not please me well enough, you and the men may have use of her. Oh, and have this mess cleaned up. Hang the bodies over the main gate, to remind these scum who is master here, in Perugia."

"The locals will not bother us," Valdo sneers. "They are all old women, and have no courage."

"Even the lowest dog needs a kick, now and then," the condottiero replies. "Take her away."

The girl shakes, and sobs, as she is forcibly dragged across the courtyard, and thrown into a tower room. As the key turns in the lock, Valdo explains that he will be second, after his condottiero has finished with her. She slumps to the floor, and begins to cry.

With her entire family dead, there is only one thing left to her, as a good Italian girl, and that is, in her heart, to swear *vendetta* against the condottiero, and his men. Then she realises that to obtain her revenge, she must remain alive. This means that she must either please the animal Baglioni in bed, or escape at once.

*

She waits for dusk. The door is firmly locked, and the window is very small. She twists, and turns, until the upper part of her body his through, then catches hold of the sturdy vine growing up the tower wall, and pulls herself free. Then she slithers down the vine that hugs the ancient tower's wall, to the ground. Then she picks up her skirts, looks to see no guards are about, and runs for her life.

Once in the huddle of streets surrounding the main citadel, Pippa can hide, and get her breath back. After she regains her strength, she works her way out into the open countryside, helped by a few of the sympathetic townsfolk, who risk death by giving her food, and directions.

She knows her father has misled Malatesta Baglioni, and that there is no grand army coming to invade, but there is a smaller force, due to make an incisive raid. She resolves to keep walking, until she finds them, and can tell them all that she knows.

Pippa Micheletto cannot draw a sword, and fight her sworn enemy, but she can help to bring him down, and gain some sort of revenge. The moon is full, and she walks throughout the night, putting many miles between her, and the traitorous condottiero.

*

"A beautiful sight, signor," the Venetian escort's captain says. Thomas

Wyatt looks at the splendour of Rome, spreading out before him, and shrugs.

"I have been here before, Antonio," he says. "I was not made welcome then, and I doubt things have changed over much. The Pope still dances to the emperor's tune, and the city's god is still Mammon."

"Then I hope you have plenty of gold," Antonio replies, chuckling. "For Clement is a rapacious dog, and will want every ducat you have, and more."

"I have no gold with me," the poet says. "I come with a letter from your Doge, which will get me an audience, and two messages from my master, Thomas Cromwell."

"Is this *Tomas* Cromwell a great man in England?"

"Some would think so, and some not," Wyatt replies, candidly. "For every man who calls him friend, there is one who would call him a cur. Great men attract great enemies."

"Why will Clement listen to *your* great man?" Antonio is curious, as politics in Italy usually involves either huge amounts of gold, or sudden, violent death. "Does he fear him?"

"My master does not make threats," Wyatt concludes, spurring his horse on. "He simply asks."

"*Cristo Santo!*" young Antonio exclaims, galloping after his charge. "Without gold, he might as well whistle out of his *culo*."

Thomas Wyatt does not hear. He is a hundred yards ahead, recounting, in his mind, how he will speak to Pope Clement on the morrow. As a member of the hated, and feared Medici family, he will be a shrewd bargainer, and a hard man to scare.

Even with the two powerful weapons at his disposal, the poet might still fail. He curses, and wishes that it was Cromwell here, in his position, and able to converse directly with the king's worst enemy. Not for the first time, Wyatt wonders what the price of failure will be.

Will Draper, Mush, Richard, and himself will be banished from Henry's court, probably for ever, but Thomas Cromwell might well pay a far greater price. Fail tomorrow, and the poet could be condemning the Privy Councillor to death. It is hard to contemplate such an end, and Wyatt pushes the thought from his mind.

Then he is at one of the city's many gates, and two guards are approaching him. He recalls the last time, when he had fought his way out, and is relieved when Antonio and his men gallop up, and demand entry.

"On the business of Andrea Gritti, Doge of the Free City State of Venice, you dog!"

There is nothing, Thomas Wyatt thinks to himself, like a little diplomacy. He half expects the guards to be awkward, but Antonio judges the situation well, and knows they will be scared of refusing admission, and incurring the wrath of Clement, the Medici Bishop of Rome. They wave them through.

They are within the city, and the poet's heart is moved at the sight of so much decaying magnificence. Great buildings glisten in the sun, alongside crumbling ruins, and huddles of private villas. It seems to the poet that the wealth of the world must reside within these walls, and he can easily see how such a city once ruled the whole world, from far off Cathay, to the north of Britain.

"Tonight, we lodge with Signor Franconi, a rich wool merchant, and a friend of your master."

"He knows Cromwell?"

"Of course," Antonio says, with a glint in his eye. "Everyone knows *Tomas* Cromwell!"

7   Intrigue in Rome

"An Englishman?" Pope

Clement asks, as he finishes off his breakfast. "That dirty *stronzo,* Gritti, wishes me to grant an Englishman an immediate audience?"

"He does, Your Holiness," the Papal Chamberlain says, persuasively. "It seems the man has something of great import to tell you. The Doge writes, saying he knows what this Signor Wyatt will say, and urges you to listen, at your earliest moment."

"Why should we listen to the Doge?" Clement asks. "He hates my family, and does not love Mother Church. Why, he will not even visit the Papal Court."

"Your predecessor *did* try to poison *his* predecessor, Your Holiness," the chamberlain reminds his master. "Had he succeeded in the task, things might have been otherwise, but it did not work, and we must accept his distrust. The Doge is insistent that the Englishman is heard, as it will bring great benefit to both our states."

"The insolent swine," Clement says. "he'll think otherwise, when our condottiero, Baglioni, takes Padua from him."

"As the Doge does not know our plans, might I suggest we humour him, and let him think we have granted his wish?" the chamberlain says. He spends his days trying to divert his master onto the right path, and not one that is governed purely by family hatred, and revenge. "Listen to the Englishman, then send him on his way, thinking well of us. Let him report to Andrea Gritti, and put him at ease also. Then …"

"Yes. You are right, as always, my old friend," Clement replies. "Make him first … no, second audience today. "I want to speak with Donna Malaposso first. She wants a knighthood for her husband, and I am disposed to lend my help."

"She is a generous woman, Your Holiness," the chamberlain says. The Pope is only in his early fifties, and still needs the consolation of the flesh. "Shall I allow an hour?"

"That will suffice," Clement says, "unless she is *very* grateful indeed."

Then I shall present the Englishman at eleven. His name is Thomas Wyatt. He was here with the Duke of Bedford, a few years back."

"Ah, yes. Poor Bedford was captured by the emperor's men, and held to ransom. They were bad times." Clement rises, and moves into the centre of the huge room. Immediately, four servants rush forward, and start to dress him for the day. "I do hope that Gritti's friend will not be too tiresome."

*

Thomas Wyatt bows low to the lady emerging from the Pope's throne room. She curtseys back at him, and is about to move on, when she pauses, and smiles at the poet.

"*Tomas?*" she asks.

"Donna Maria Vutti," Wyatt says, and takes her hand.

"Donna Maria Malaposso now, you naughty boy," she says. "What ever happened to you?"

"I was taken captive, on my way to visit you," Wyatt lies, smoothly. "I fled the city, and this is the first time I could return, safely, my dearest Maria."

"Why are you here, now?"

"To speak with the Pope."

"You will find him in a good mood," the courtesan says. "I have just this moment relieved his anxieties."

"He is a Medici, and must have many."

"You are as sharp tongued as ever," she replies. "Come, I will take you in, and ask him to look upon you with favour." Before he can answer, Maria sweeps back into the Papal throne room. "My dearest Giulio, look who is here to see you. A dear old friend of mine, from

England."

Clement is embarrassed at her using his given name, but can forgive her anything. Maria Malaposso, despite being almost forty, is still the most desirable woman in Rome. He beckons them both forward, and dismisses his chamberlain.

"You must forgive me keeping you waiting, Signor Wyatt," he says, holding out his ring hand. Tom Wyatt steps forward, and kisses the magnificent Papal ring. "I was just … listening to this lady's confession."

"Adding to my sins, more like," Maria announces. "Drop the act, Giulio, *Tomas* is an even greater goat than you. Invite us to lunch, and I will gather a few *gnocca*; or would you prefer a *troia* or two, Your Holiness?"

Thomas Wyatt smiles at the Popes discomfort. Maria is an expensive woman, and *gnocca* and *troia* are varying degrees of whore. One is paid with silver, and the other with a couple of copper coins.

"You wicked little slut," Pope Clement says, shrugging his shoulders, as if in surrender. "Very well, whistle up a few more nice girls, and let us celebrate with Master Wyatt."

"Celebrate what, Your Holiness?" the poet asks.

"What ever it is you are here to tell me," he replies, with a mocking smile. "Maria vouches for you, and says you are a great … what is the word in English? No matter. We will see, young man."

*

The meal, which started at noon is showing no signs of coming to a close, despite it being late afternoon. Maria, true to her word, returns with three more women, and strews them about the dining room. Wine is plentiful, and of the most excellent quality, and the Pope drinks vast amounts, with no apparent effect. Between courses, he fondles one or another of the girls, and invites Thomas Wyatt to do the same.

"Is he always like this?" Wyatt whispers in Maria's ear, when she comes, and sits on his knee, staking her claim for the evening, at least.

"Since they sacked Rome," she replies. "He is frightened of losing everything, so spends his days playing at politics, and proving his manhood with one of the courtesans, or even a common street whore."

"And you?"

"I keep him at arms length," Maria tells him. "Until I want a favour. It keeps him keen. You aren't going to hurt him, are you?"

"Not I," Tom Wyatt says. "Though he might be better off leaving the Venetians alone. Why does he covet Padua?"

"Baglioni bullies him into action," Maria explains. "He promises a united Italy, under the Pope. The man is a scoundrel."

"So I hear." Wyatt sees that Clement is watching, so kisses the woman on his knee, and strokes her thigh. "Will he not be jealous?"

"I doubt it," says Maria. "He will touch, and he will fondle, but the girls will go home unmolested. Poor Giulio boasts much, and does little. He is like a castrato, since Rome fell to the emperor. We play up to him, and tell wild stories of how he satisfies us, two and three at a time. He pays well for it."

"Dear God," Wyatt says. "Are you still at the same house?"

"No, I am married now, and live near the Palatine, in a new villa. Anyone can tell you how to find me."

"What of your husband?"

"Away, with Baglioni's army."

"Then I shall pay my respects, tonight."

"All night, I trust?" Maria says.

"You shall have my undivided attention," Wyatt promises. "Now, can

137

you remove your friends, and let me talk with Clement?"

"Call him Giulio. He prefers it, when he's been drinking."

The room clears, and Tom Wyatt moves to sit alongside the Pope. He takes a fold of parchment from his doublet, and places it in front of His Holiness.

"My letters of introduction, Giulio," he says.

"Where are the girls?" Giulio asks.

"You have worn them out, sir," Wyatt tells him. "Now, we can talk. I have two proposals for you. My master says that you must choose which ever suits you best."

"Your master?"

"Master Thomas Cromwell, the King of England's most favoured Privy Councillor, sir."

"Ah, I know of Cromwell. He is Wolsey's man."

"Cardinal Wolsey is dead, Giulio," Wyatt reminds him.

"Yes, of course. Was he poisoned?"

"No, he died in bed, of ... a broken heart."

"A fine man, who might have succeeded me, one day," the Pope says. "Still, I am sure Cromwell is as capable.

What does he offer me?"

"He is charged, by François, King of France, to find a husband, for his illegitimate daughter, Marie. It is for Master Cromwell to choose, and he is minded of your own son, born out of wedlock, and wonders if a match might be made."

"He has the power?"

"He promises François, a hundred thousand pounds, and the girl is bought," Tom Wyatt explains. "Say the word, and it is a love match. They shall be betrothed at once, and married, the moment you conclude your part of the bargain."

"Ha! A bargain. here comes the devil, to spit in our face. You wish me to betray the emperor?"

"Not at all. You are looking into the matter of the king's annulment and…"

"Never!" The part of Giulio Medici that remains Pope Clement knows he must refuse even this magnificent bribe. His greatest wish in life is to see his son married into one of the great royal families. "I shall never allow Henry to buy an annulment."

"We understand this," Tom Wyatt continues, smoothly, "and wish nothing more than for you to come to a swift decision… even if it is *not* in Henry's favour."

"What, you want me to refuse your king?" The Medici is wrong footed for a moment.

"That is your intention, is it not?" Wyatt asks. "You want this marriage, and we want a decision. All you have to do, is announce that you find against King Henry, and your son will marry a French princess."

"I could always delay my decision, until your king is too old to sire other children. Then Emperor Charles will favour me." The Pope sees it all, and will not have any of the plan. "You seek a path that will lead Henry away from Rome."

"That is not your concern, sir," Wyatt says. "Although, there is a second offer, that you might find most interesting. Master Cromwell calls it 'the French option', and is considering it, even as we speak."

"What is this second choice?" Giulio Medici is suspicious, and is quite right to be so. The second offer is not going to be to his taste, at all.

"Master Cromwell will have Queen Katherine strangled, and give it out that it was because of your stubbornness to negotiate. The emperor's favourite aunt will be dead, at your instigation. How friendly will Charles be then, my friend?"

"You would not do such a thing," Clement says. "It is monstrous."

"No, I would not," Tom Wyatt tells him, "but there is no shortage of willing helpers. Cromwell's nephew, Richard, is a great beast of a man, and will snap her neck in a trice."

"On your sacred honour, Master Wyatt ... Cromwell would do such a thing?"

"If he does not hear by twelfth night, Queen Katherine, aunt of the emperor, will die," Wyatt tells him. "It is a drastic solution, but one forced on us, by you, Your Holiness."

"I must think. I don't know what to do, or ..."

"Take the first option, sir." Tom Wyatt places a comforting hand on Giulio Medici's shoulder. "Everyone will be happy. Your son, the French princess, you, and my own king. Even the Emperor Charles will be relieved that it is done with."

"But the damage..." Clement is a husk of a man, and can hardly think straight anymore. The Medici side of him is all that keeps him going.

"What sort of damage can there be?" Thomas Wyatt tells his greatest lie. "Afterwards, if the king strays too far from the church, you can threaten to excommunicate him. He is a pious man, and will not let that happen. Henry will come to Rome, and kiss your ring, rather than break with Mother Church. Then he will gladly burn a few heretics, and celebrate the birth of many strong sons."

"You are right, my friend," the Pope says. "I see that clearly now. Then the deal is struck?"

"Almost," Tom Wyatt says. He is the consummate diplomat, and always has a parting shot. "You must withdraw your support of Malatesta Baglioni, at once."

"He will be furious with me," the Pope says, almost whining. "I am frightened of what he will do."

"Nothing, sir. There is an army of thirty thousand, moving out of Venice, even now. Baglioni is a dead man. Cut him loose, and save your face."

"Very well, but for God's sake, do not let him live, or we are all doomed!"

"Can one man inspire so much fear?" Wyatt asks. "He will never dare harm the Pope."

"He is not a man," Clement says, almost whispering. "It is said that he has forged a deal with the devil. He drinks the blood of virgins, and does Satan's bidding. In return, he is more than a mortal man. It is said that no blade can pierce him. How can he die?"

"Pull yourself together, Your Holiness," Tom Wyatt tells him. "I am English, so I do not believe in the devil. I have a man with me who will destroy Baglioni. Now, call your chamberlain, so that we can draw up the documents. Henry must be refused, forthwith!"

*

"Good day to you, Master Cromwell," Tom Audley says, stamping the snow from his boots at the door to Austin Friars. "The weather has turned, I see."

"A mere flurry, Tom," A genial sounding Cromwell replies, ushering him inside. "I have a warm fire going. Come and sit a while, and tell me how Parliament went this morning."

Tom Audley, one of the king's favoured councillors, and a sitting Member of Parliament throws off his fur lined cloak, and accepts a cup of hot, spiced wine.

"There was some talk of discussing the king's business by several members from Northamptonshire, and the West Country, but it was shouted down by the Duke of Suffolk's men. I guess he arranged it at your instigation?"

Cromwell raises an eyebrow, but does not answer.

"What then?"

"It will go as you wish, Master Cromwell." Audley cannot help but admire how the man manages to arrange matters, with a word, here and there. "The third session was a shambles, and the new member for Putney suggested we adjourn. On a show of hands, we agreed to postpone the session, until the middle of January, 1532."

"Excellent, Tom," Cromwell says. "This will give us time to frame the new laws better, and work things to our advantage."

"Providing you get the answer you want from Rome," Tom Audley says. "What if Wyatt fails?"

"Then we find another way," Cromwell replies, "but come what may, I will force a split with the Bishop of Rome, and make Henry the true head of the English church."

"Henry is scared of excommunication."

"True, but he loves money." Cromwell takes Audley to his desk, and shows him a ledger. "See here. This is a list of revenues, going to the monastic institutions, the churches, and the abbeys and priories of England and Wales. So far, it totals almost a million pounds, most of which then goes to Rome."

"God in Heaven!" Audley whistles under his breath. "Are these figures true?"

"You doubt me?"

"Of course not," Audley says, hurriedly. "It is just that the figures are so massive. Why, the whole country only brings in a million to the royal treasury."

"This will double it," Cromwell continues. "The new laws, once ratified, will divert this money to the English crown, who will return a tenth of it to the churches, for their minimal upkeep. Let any object, and it is treason."

"Making Henry the head of the church, within England is a shrewd move," Audley confesses. "If the monks wish to go over his head, then it must be to God alone, and not Clement in Rome. I was wondering about the treasure."

"Treasure?" Cromwell smiles benignly at his favourite Parliamentarian. "What treasure?"

"Well, if Henry is head of the church in England, everything within the church belongs to him," Audley explains. "From the silver chalices, to the holy relics. All become the property of the ruling monarch, does it not?"

"Audley, you are a clever man," Cromwell says. Later, if the king feels he is being too harsh, he can point to the stripping away of the golden crosses, and silver goblets, and claim that Audley came up with the idea. In fact, he is already valuing each religious house, and knows that Canterbury alone will bring in almost two hundred thousand pounds of treasure. "That is something which I should have thought of. I will tell the king of your splendid idea, and ask him to let you take the task on."

"Thank you, Cromwell," Audley says, feeling rather pleased with himself. "How are things with the family? Is our young Miriam coping without her husband?"

"She is a good wife, and a fine woman of business," Cromwell tells his colleague. "She will be earning a thousand a year the way she is going!"

"A thousand a year?" Tom Audley is astounded. "I trust she invests it wisely. I can always talk to some of my people in Antwerp."

"She has her own," Cromwell says, boasting about her, as if she were his own daughter. "In Antwerp, in Paris, and in Bruges. I hear she is also looking at opening up trade in the north. She is forging close links with the Chester business community. Something to do with cheese."

"You must be proud," Audley

says. "I pray that her husband is as successful, and we get the answer we want from Rome."

"Let us drink to it," Tom Cromwell says, picking up his hot spiced wine. "Here's to a speedy conclusion to their business, and a safe return for Tom Wyatt, and his party."

"Ah, then you have not heard?" Thomas Audley saves the worst news to last.

"What is it?"

"The Lord Chancellor."

"Oh, poor dear Thomas More," Cromwell says, shaking his head. "What is he up to now?"

"He is content searching out these pamphleteers," Audley tells Cromwell. "They think it funny to make up rude ditties about the Pope, or the new Bishop of Winchester. He smashes the printing press, and has them flogged in public. It seems to give him some pleasure. Now and then, one is mad enough to rhyme Harry, or Hal with some dirty word, and the Lord Chancellor can have him burned at the stake, or flayed alive, before beheading the poor swine."

"What is this to me?" Cromwell asks. "I can help those who hold certain religious views, but not those who traduce the king."

"One of these fools decided that it would be funny to tell the tale of a certain lady, who has been raised in Paris, before coming to London. It hints that she is very fond of *amour*, as the French say, and describes in the filthiest detail what she likes doing, with a string of eager lovers."

"Dear Christ," Tom Cromwell slumps into a chair. "Tell me the worst."

"The lady is obviously Anne Boleyn, but the 'lovers' are well disguised, all except for one, a poet, who is called Tim Whatnot."

"Baron Montagu," Cromwell hisses. "He seeks a crude revenge on me. He cannot make a head on attack, for I have ruined him time and again, so he does this."

"Worse than that. A copy was sent to Sir Thomas More, anonymously, of course. It did not take him long to deduce who Master Whatnot is, and what is inferred. I hear that he took it to Henry, along with a few other pamphlets. The king, though he always expresses shock at the content, does like to have a read through the ruder ones."

"Cleverly done," Cromwell sighs. It is how he would have handled it, letting the king come upon it, as if by accident, and expressing horror at his interpretation. 'Surely not, sire', and 'I can scarcely believe it', would be apt phrases to employ. I can just imagine Henry's reaction."

"He went purple." Audley grasps his own throat, as if to mime the act of having a fit. "It was bad enough to see his sweet lady love made out to be nothing but a cheap French whore, but when he recognised Tom Wyatt, he almost burst asunder with rage. Sir Thomas became most apologetic, and swore he had not understood it to mean either Lady Anne, or Thomas Wyatt ... though he did manage to recall that they had been schooled together in earlier times."

"Clever." Cromwell strokes his chin. "You were there then, my friend?"

"I was. I stepped in to the fray, and declared the entire thing to be nothing but a filthy tissue of lies. I said that no sane man would ever think such a disgusting thing of Lady Anne. I swore that, to my own knowledge, Wyatt has been abroad more than in England, these last three years."

"Was he calmed by your words?"

"Partly. I reminded him that it was Tom Wyatt who fought alongside Will Draper against the Welsh rebels, and helped save us from civil war."

"Well said, Audley," Cromwell

comments. "What then?"

"More agrees, but reminds the king that it was Cromwell men he fought alongside, and that his father is a friend of your good self."

"My old friend has a venomous tongue. What then befell?"

"Henry declares the whole thing treasonous, and says that the culprit must be found, given a fair trial, and then be boiled alive."

"Oh, well done, Master Audley," Cromwell says, regaining his composure. "Then he does not suspect Tom Wyatt?"

"Not of having intercourse with Lady Anne, sir, but certainly of something."

"What?"

"He knows not, but seems to think one can be guilty, without the other. As if Wyatt simply wishing to have Anne Boleyn is a crime."

"But it is," Thomas Cromwell says, "Any act, whether by deed, or thought, against the king, is now deemed to be treason. A stray thought can lose you your head. I am afraid that Tom Wyatt is walking on eggshells. What was the conclusion?"

"More, in that self righteous way of his, wants to investigate, but I told Henry that it will look bad. The Lord

Chancellor of England, looking into Lady Anne's past, and then linking her to a well known ribald poet... unthinkable. People will gossip, and cast a shadow over his relationship with her. He agreed with my view, and asked me to look into it instead."

"Then we have time to repair the damage," Thomas Cromwell says. "Henry must be made to see it is all a nonsense, or Tom Wyatt will end up on the scaffold."

"He may end up on one anyway," says Tom Audley, "for Henry is becoming suspicious of everyone, these days. I wonder who is safe, and who not."

"We must not wonder, my friend," Cromwell tells his colleague. "We must direct the king's attention away from those we wish to preserve, and focus it on those who mean us harm."

"You mean the Lord Chancellor?"

"Does he have any love for us?" Cromwell asks. "He wishes to pull me down, and with me, all my friends. He wants both pope and king conjoined again, and for every non-conformist to be promptly burnt at the stake."

"He is a powerful man, Thomas," Audley replies. "Perhaps more powerful than Wolsey was. He is a formidable enemy."

"His weakness is his self belief." Cromwell finishes his drink. "He is so convinced he knows what is right for England, that he forgets something important. It must be right for Henry and Anne… not England. He is out of favour with Lady Anne, and on thin ice with the king. We must crack that ice, Tom, and let the man sink."

"If we lose," Audley says, "then we lose our heads."

"If we lose," Cromwell responds, "England will lose *its* head."

"May God help us."

"May God help Tom Wyatt and Will Draper," Cromwell concludes. "The fate of England rests on them."

8   Temptation

There are fires burning along the ferry landing when Tom Wyatt canters up.

He has ridden hard from Rome, and is eager to be back with his friends. There are more guards than usual, and the ferry boat men are feeding the flames with driftwood, and lumps of charcoal. He dismounts, and walks towards the first free boat.

"Your business, signor?" the captain of the guard asks.

"I am an English emissary, with urgent documents, for the Doge. I was hoping to get a boat, even at this late an hour. I will pay double, if any man will take me out onto the lagoon."

"Where do you come from?" the captain asks.

"From Rome," Wyatt replies, beginning to wonder at the sudden tightening of security. "I have come from Pope Clement, and have news of His Holiness."

"Not from Milan, or Lombardy then?"

"No, captain," the poet says. "Is there some trouble? Is Venice under attack from that quarter?"

"I have orders that no traveller is to reach Venice, if he has been travelling through Milan, or has stayed in Lombardy, these last few days. It is the plague, signor. It is in Constantinople once more, and comes from the north, and by sea. We had to sink a ship, and turn away others that carry the disease."

"Dear God, is it in the city?"

"Not yet. The Doge acted quickly, and we might yet be spared." The captain has a young wife, and two children, and dreads what may happen if the *lenticulae* spreads to the island state again.

Tom Wyatt understands now why the fires burn. It is to try and repulse the ill humours that carry the disease. He sees that there is an added urgency to his mission, and an added danger. It is one thing to be stabbed in the heat of battle, or cut down by a jealous husband, but death at the hands of an invisible enemy would be unspeakable.

"Have one of these fellows untie his boat, captain," Tom Wyatt says. "Here is a purse of silver coins for your trouble."

"Keep your money for the moment, signor. I will get you to Venice tonight, if you would but do me one favour. My name is Giovanni Ipolatto, and I live in the married quarters at the city's main barracks. Deliver the coins to my wife, and tell her I am well, and will return, once the danger is past."

"I will do this small thing for you, Captain Ipolatto," Tom Wyatt promises. "Are you banned from the city

154

too?"

"I am, along with the Doge's entire Swiss guard, and some hundreds of gentlemen, who choose to stay in camp on the mainland."

"Is there an Englishman with them?" Wyatt asks.

"Four," the captain confirms. "They are crazy, of course. The one who is a soldier talks about us winning. He says he has never yet lost a battle. Is this so?"

"It is," Tom Wyatt confirms. "Except to his wife."

"*Naturelmente!*" Giovanni Ipolatto says, and they both laugh at the unsubtle jest. To lose such a battle as marriage is inevitable.

*

"How was your journey?" The Doge is seated on an ivory throne, picking at a plate of fish in some kind of white sauce. Thomas Wyatt bows, and produces the documents from the Papal Court. He hands them to Pietro, the Doge's castrato servant, who passes them on to his master.

"His Holiness Pope Clement the Seventh, sends his blessings to you, My Lord Doge, and pledges his eternal friendship."

"*Stronzo*," the Doge curses. He sees beyond the shallow flattery, uttered by his enemy, Giulio Medici, and can barely contain his disgust. "He shits lies, and was vomited up by a bitch. Is he well, my friend?"

"I fear not," Tom Wyatt says, surprised at the vehemence of the Doge's response. "He appears liverish, and suffers from a variety of minor ailments."

"Does he have the French disease?" Andrea Gritti asks. "Or is he too feeble to lie with women these days?"

"You are right, sir," the poet responds. "He is feeble, and can do nothing but pander, and drink wine to excess. I was rather shocked."

"It is a Medici failing," the Doge replies, smiling. "He will die of either drink, or the pox, before long. Then we will need a new pope. You must tell Cromwell to suggest a good candidate."

"I asked him to give an answer, concerning the king's marriage, My Lord."

"And he said he would consider the request, but that it was a weighty matter, and might take some time to decide." The Doge shakes his head, sure he has predicted Pope Clement's reply correctly.

"No, sir, he did not," Tom Wyatt says, gesturing to the folded document, authenticated with the Vatican's seal. "He will make an announcement presently, refusing the king's request, and threatening him with excommunication, unless he returns to Queen Katherine."

"Then you are a master diplomat," the Doge says, reaching for the papers. "You have succeeded in ruining your king's chances, for all time. Do you still wish me to support the Pope's decision?"

"Of course." Tom Wyatt is merely the instrument, used by Cromwell, but he can admire the cleverness of it all. "You must, 'with regret' agree with the Papal decision. The king will have no other choice than to cast Clement aside, and take his own road."

"Cromwell's road, you mean." The Doge nods his understanding. "I see what my old friend is up to, and hope he succeeds. To set Henry against Rome is a dangerous thing to do, and most of the world will be against him. Does he mean there to be a complete break?"

"I believe so, Your Majesty."

"I am not a majesty, Master Wyatt," Andrea Gritti says. "I am but the chosen leader of the Senate. I have little time left, and must leave Venice in a better state than from when I became Doge. You must tell Will Draper that the time is near."

"Gladly, sir," Wyatt replies. He has left the best news until the last, as any good diplomat should. "Pope Clement tells me that he will break with Malatesta Baglioni, and will not support him if he moves against either Padua, or Venice."

"Then the Roman army will stay put," Gritti says, with a hint of triumph in his voice. He recalculates swiftly, and alters his plans in the blink of an eye. "That means Baglioni must rely solely on his own forces. I will send word to Florence, and Siena, where we have good friends. Siena will close the city gates to Baglioni, and declare for Venice."

"What of Florence?"

"A Medici rules there, but my agents will try and keep him neutral, if nothing else. He is Clement's son, as I am sure you know."

"Will the condottiero split his army to deal with them?" Tom Wyatt is calculating the odds. "If he sends troops to lay siege to both towns, his army will be halved."

"Yes, and I have spread rumours, saying our fleet of fifty galleons will raid the Umbrian coast, and take Rimini from him. With luck, this condottiero will spread himself far too thinly."

"If a strong force were to strike at Perugia, it might be able to take the city, and leave Baglioni isolated, fighting on three, or four, fronts at once." Thomas Wyatt thinks he sees it all clearly, and is letting his enthusiasm get the better of his common sense.

"There is one problem," the Doge says. "I do not have fifty galleons. I have three, and one of them is not yet seaworthy. Then again, Florence and Siena may surrender at the first sight of one of Baglioni's brigands. We weave illusions, my boy, and hope the magic works."

"Then Will Draper might find himself up against a host of men." Tom Wyatt frowns. "I must join him tomorrow. He will need every man he can raise."

"He has my Swiss guard, and every young blade in Venice, and the Veneto," the Doge tells the poet. "Why, I am told that he even has my zoologist!"

"Does he have cannon?"

"I'm afraid not."

"You have cannon here, do you not?" Tom Wyatt recalls seeing some upon their arrival. "Down by the waterfront. I saw a brace of the things."

"We have two cannon, captured from the French almost fifty years ago. I doubt they will work."

"Let us try them out, My Lord," the poet says. "If they work, we can hoist them onto a couple of carts, and take them into battle."

"We have no shot," Pietro, the effeminate castrato pipes up.

"In England, we are trying out a new method, invented by the French," Wyatt replies. "One must load a chain, with a weight at each end. It stretches out, when discharged, and acts like a scythe."

"Dear Christ in Heaven!" the ageing Doge says, crossing himself. "What ever will they think of next?"

*

"I must return to Chester tomorrow," Ned Small says, toying with the food on his pewter plate. The tavern, on the outer reaches of Putney is not renowned for its cuisine, but it is secluded, and has private rooms. "My father is ill, and he needs me."

"He will be pleased with the business you have done for him in London," Miriam tells him. "We shall all benefit from the arrangement."

"What of *our* arrangement?" Ned says, placing his hand over hers. "You know my heart is yours."

"Do not talk like that," Miriam says. She is not surprised by his words, and even finds them flattering. "I am a married woman."

"Whose husband is abroad,

doing who knows what?" Ned replies, persuasively. "Months away from you, and seemingly without a second thought. What kind of man is that?"

"Will is a wonderful man, and a fine husband to me," Miriam tells him, but she does feel a little resentment at his absence. "I am not one to break my wedding vows, Ned."

"I understand, but what about him?" Ned says, pressing home his advantage. The husband is not here to defend himself, and the young man is much taken with his new business partner. "He is a soldier of fortune, who takes his share of the spoils. If that share includes women, captured after some brawl, will he take his pick? In the heat of battle, the blood is hot, and men behave badly, without thinking. Might he not sate his lusts, and think to repent afterwards?"

"My husband is decent, and honest. If he ever does wrong, it is because it is the lesser of two evils," Miriam says. "You merely blacken his name to further your case with me."

"Say you do not want me," Ned presses on. "Tell me you do not find me handsome."

"I cannot, for it would be a lie," Miriam confesses. "My heart fluttered when we shook hands the other day, and after dinner, I was loath to let you go from me, when Master Cromwell left. Had you pressed me then, I fear I might have given myself to you."

"Then more fool I, for not realising it then," Ned Small tells her. "I am a decent fellow, and I too am honest. Say the word, and I will swear my love, and spend as much time as I can in London. If you cannot leave your husband, I beg you, share your love between us. I am willing to stay in the background, taking your favours only when I may. Your husband need never know."

"You would do that?"

"And more. Stay with your husband, and let me become your lover. I will settle for that."

"You confuse me, Ned. Your words make me want to … to hold you, and find comfort with you."

"Then I shall take a room, and we can seal our love."

"Love?" The word pierces the fog of indecision surrounding Miriam. "What you propose is not love, Ned. It is simple lust. The twining together of two animals. I cannot rush into such a thing. I must go, and think this through. If I do come to you, it must be honestly. Do you understand what I mean?"

"Yes, you need a little time," Ned says, "but you will come to me?"

"I will," Miriam says, firmly. "I will renounce my vows, and ask Master Cromwell to obtain a divorce for me, from the Pope. Then I will explain to my husband, the moment he returns from killing his enemies, that you are now my lover. I do hope he takes it in good part. Will has a tendency to kill first, and ask questions later. Still, what of that? True love will always win out, and we will have a few tender weeks before his return."

"You want to leave your husband?" Ned Small can feel his limbs begin to shake. "I sought only to ... make an arrangement, whereby we might ..."

"Fornicate behind his back?" Miriam asks. Her moment of madness is past, and she cannot understand what she sees in the young man, who is a pale imitation of her husband.

"Well... yes." Ned is deflated. He realises that Miriam has no intention of sleeping with him, and does not know what to say. "I thought it might be quite pleasurable. Have I offended you?"

"By finding me attractive?" Miriam smiles. "No, I am not offended, though I am surprised that so clever tongued a fellow is still unwed."

"Ah, yes. Well, the fact of the matter is … I have three children, and am a little bit married."

"A little bit?" Miriam laughs out loud. "Is that not like being a little bit pregnant, or a little bit dead? Oh, you incorrigible rogue, what will I do with you?"

"If you will not bed me, then forgive me," Ned says, regaining his confidence. "I do not want your husband killing me for nothing other than admiring his wife."

"I fear my brother would be first in line," Miriam tells him. "He has the hot bloodedness of our race."

"Your race?"

"Yes, my people are from Coventry," the girl says, smiling. She cannot help but like Ned Small, and will not throw away a good business deal just because he admires her. Besides, she thinks, what if Will were ever put to the test? Can he remain faithful, for months on end?

She takes her leave, and makes her way back to her house on the river. Behind, a lone figure pays his bill, and follows. The young man, detailed to keep a watchful eye on Miriam will report back, as he does each evening, that Mistress Miriam Draper has passed an exemplary day, conducting business, and running her household.

*

Pippa Micheletto can feel the hard road through her worn shoes, and her feet are burning. She has covered almost thirty miles, on foot, avoiding fellow travellers, and hoping, against hope to stumble on the great Venetian army as it approaches.

She knows her father lied to Baglioni, but is sure that some sort of force is coming. Her father died, tricking the condottiero into believing a mighty force was assembling, and his lies saved her life. Once having climbed out of the window of the tower, however, she was on her own.

"Bread?" The tall man appears from the cover of some bushes, and is suddenly in front of her. She steps back, and looks which way to run. The Umbrian countryside is a lawless place, and Pippa knows that a young girl alone is easy prey. The man sees she is prepared to run, and taps the chain about his neck. There is a jewelled crucifix hanging on it. "I am Father … Geraldo. You need have no fear of me, girl. Come. Eat, and we will go on together. You should not be alone. Where are your parents?"

"Dead." It is a simple admission,

and she feels tears coming. The priest sighs, and presses the piece of bread into her hand. Then he turns, and waits for her to fall in beside him. "Thank you for this kindness, father."

"There are those abroad who would even offer violence to a priest," Father Geraldo says. "Are you armed?"

"No, father."

"Here, take this." The priest conjures a thin stiletto from his wide sleeved garment, and hands it to her. "Hide it in the folds of your dress. Do not be afraid to use it."

They walk on. The priest is walking to Venice, which he explains, is a penance, placed on him by his bishop.

"I spoke out about something I should not," he says. "Bishop Bennotti decided to punish me. I must walk to Venice, with a note for the Cardinal of the Veneto. It will ask the cardinal to send me back to Rome, on foot. My bishop has a keen sense of humour. What is your tale, little one?"

Pippa tells the priest about being taken by Baglioni's men, and of how her father was tortured, and made to watch as her brother, and her step mother were murdered. She does not mention the fact that her father was a Venetian spy, but concludes by saying she is in search of friends of her father, who will help her gain her revenge.

"Vendetta will ruin you, child," the priest says. "Even if you succeed, those you kill will have friends, who will come for you."

"I cannot give up, father," she says.

"What's this?" A big, dirty looking rogue appears from behind a tree. "Why, it's a priest, with his daughter. You dirty old swine. Or is she your mistress, old man?"

"Step aside, my son," the priest says. "This child is under my protection, and I am under God's."

"Then I hope he can fight," the man says. Two more men come out of the hedgerow, each carrying a cudgel. The first man draws a knife. "A fair trade, priest. We'll give you your life, in return for your purse, and this girl. Have you broken her in yet?"

"I warn you..."

"No, father," Pippa says, stepping towards the big man. "It is only fair, and I will be safer with these men, once they have had what they want. Am I right sir?"

"Good girl," he says. "We will make you happier than the priest can. God's teeth!" Pippa's knife slashes up, opening a great gash from the man's wrist to his shoulder. He staggers back, clutching at the horrible wound. The other two are startled for a moment, then run forward. Father Geraldo draws a short sword from beneath his cloak, and charges.

One man tries to knock the priest down with his cudgel, but he steps aside, and stabs at the man's unguarded chest. The man drops his weapon and clutches at his side. The third man is already running for his life. Father Geraldo sheathes his sword, and goes over to the leader. He examines the wound, which is pumping out blood, shakes his head, and starts to administer the last rites.

"Oh, God, am I done for," the man says, slipping into the final sleep. "Done, by a girl."

The priest stands, and goes over to the other wounded man, who has already lapsed into unconsciousness. The priest's sword thrust has collapsed a lung, and pierced his heart. In moments, as the priest prays for his soul, he is dead too.

"A pity the other fellow escaped," the priest says, wiping Pippa's knife clean of blood for her. "Let us hope he has no further friends. We should find lodgings in a village."

"I have no money, father," Pippa

168

says.

"God will provide, my dear," Father Geraldo tells her. "He always does, somehow."

*

"Well, Master Quartermaster, what news have you for me?" Will Draper is crouched over a table in one of the small canvas tents which his rag tag army are using, to keep the colder Veneto nights at bay.

"I have the full tally now," Richard Cromwell says, and consults the scroll he has brought with him. "Swiss guardsmen, one hundred and ninety six, fit for duty. Mush's cavalry number four hundred and twelve, all with swords and daggers. Some men from Padua and Genoa have volunteered, but they are badly armed, and untrained. They come to another sixty four. Then there are the English contingent. Apart from we gentlemen, five in number, there are the crews of two English ships, which have been refused a landing in Venice, because of the plague. They number eighty four, including the two captains. They have some pistols, knives, and cutlasses, and look like they can manage a scrap well enough."

"A messenger from the Doge tells me that Tom Wyatt is back, and will be here tomorrow, along with two elderly cannon."

"Now we are talking," Richard says, enthusiastically. "That makes us seven hundred and sixty one men, with some pikes, a few dozen muskets, and a pair of ancient canon. The Condottiero of Perugia must be soiling himself in fear of us."

"It's enough," Will says. "Remember that God forsaken valley in Wales? Seven of us, against a hundred bloodthirsty Welsh rebels."

"It was fifty," Richard replies, "and we only won because their leader was killed early on. I doubt we can pull the same trick twice. Besides, large armies have generals, and colonels, to take over."

"You don't have to come," Will says. "In fact, it might be better if you stay behind, and report back to your uncle."

"Do you want me to strangle you?" Richard says, cracking his knuckles. "Not only will I not stay behind, I'll be first into them."

"I never doubted it, my friend." Will is curious, and has to ask Richard something that confuses him. "Tell me, how comes it that you are the gentlest of souls one moment, and a raging warrior the next. What drives you so?"

"Food," the young Cromwell tells his friend, blank faced. "I imagine that the enemy are between me, and my dinner. The thought that they might win, and eat my portion, drives me insane with anger."

"Then we must starve you before each battle," Will says.

"I am Samson," Richard says, slapping his great barrel of a chest. "Save I am weakened through lack of a nicely broiled chicken, rather than my hair!"

9   Fools and Peacocks

Autumn in England is less clement than the almost balmy days in northern Italy. The young women who maintain Austin Friars for Cromwell can smell the rain in the air, and insist on wrapping their beloved master up in his warmest, seal skin cloak. The entire ensemble is topped off with a felt hat, waterproofed with scented goose fat.

""You look nice enough to eat, Thomas," Eustace Chapuys tells his friend. "I have, as you can see, been unable to resist a display of feathers. I believe that Lady Anne is amused by my taste in caps."

"And by the obscenely large pearl earrings you sent her last week," Cromwell replies, smiling at this little man, who is now almost a fixture about the court. In short, he makes the Boleyn woman laugh, and deflects her from pressing too hard on the matter of the annulment. "La Boleyn is like any woman. She loves pretty things about her."

"Is this why you want me with you today?"

Thomas Cromwell has all but taken control of the king's complex legal and parliamentary affairs, working closely with Thomas Audley, and he has joined the inner circle of the Privy Council without any undue opposition. He is not a fool, and understands that his fellow councillors are using him as a shield between themselves, and the increasingly unstable king.

"I would be obliged, Eustace, if you could divert the lady for me,"

Cromwell tells his friend. "Tell her an amusing tale, so that I might work my magic on Henry. He is roaring thunder, and has become mindful of any man who is taller, better looking, or cleverer than he."

"Ah, you speak of Master Wyatt," Chapuys says. "I found his last verse most entertaining. You can almost feel the passion, as he writes: *Sweet nectar kisses she doth bestow, and this man's heart is all aglow, the lady fair from far flung land, but smiles, and ...*"

"Kisses Tom Wyatt's hand?" Cromwell snaps. "The fellow makes it hard for me to save his head."

"I like him, but why do you expend so much time on him, my friend?" Eustace has a suspicion that it is more than simple friendship for Wyatt's father.

"For friendship's sake," Cromwell says. In truth, he cannot allow the Spanish ambassador to know that he has an illegitimate daughter by a serving woman of old Wyatt's. Tom's father knows it all, and has kept the secret perfectly, like any true friend. In return for this, Cromwell feels obliged to keep his wayward son alive. "His father and I once had business together, and became close."

"I see. Then let us venture out

into the rain, and each fulfil our obligations." Chapuys tilts his hat to a rakish angle, and they set off. Rafe Sadler, who still, on occasion, sulks at missing out on a trip to Rome, and still regrets missing the fight against the Welsh rebels, falls in at his master's heels.

"Come, Rafe," Cromwell says, "let us make haste, and dodge the droplets!" Rafe barely manages a smile. The Privy Councillor frowns, and wonders what it will take to lighten his best young man's mood. Once Will Draper is back, he will find something interesting for young Rafe, other than constant rounds of parliamentary meetings, and audiences with the king. After all, idle hands can make mischief.

"How is Mistress Miriam faring?" Chapuys asks. He is genuinely interested in the Austin Friars clan, and feels at home in their company. "I hear she is seeing a lot of Ned Small."

"Always in public, my friend," Cromwell replies. "We are all tempted, but the best of us have their own morality. Master Small is off, back to Chester, where he will find his business interests are beginning to bear fruit. It seems a merchant in Antwerp, and another couple in Mannheim want to buy his wares. I believe he will be abroad for the next twelve months."

"Well done, Thomas," Eustace Chapuys says. "I feared he might meet with an accident."

"My first choice," Rafe Sadler says. "Strangers often lose their way in London, and end up in the river. Master Cromwell is growing softer by the day." It is the nearest Rafe can bring himself to criticise Cromwell, and he feels bad, even as the words leave his mouth. Thomas Cromwell frowns for the second time that morning.

*

"Ah, Cromwell," the king calls, as soon as he enters the inner court. "At last, an honest, simple fellow, who does not know how to flatter, or deceive. Come to me, and bring your young Master Sadler along too. I would speak with you, on a private matter."

"Your Majesty," Chapuys says, boldly. "Might I steal away your beautiful Lady Anne? I have just received a shipment of jewels, from the New World. I have stones that might add to even her beauty!" Henry nods consent, and waves his beloved Boleyn girl away.

"Go on, my pretty bird," Henry says. "Though you must not fly too far. The ambassador treats you with more love than he shows his own emperor, and I will always remember him for it."

The King, Cromwell, and Rafe Sadler, draw closer to one another, and Cromwell places his left hand on Henry's upper right arm. The contact establishes the lawyer's special status with his king, and helps the king open up his heart.

"You are troubled, Henry?" The king's eyes flicker at the familiar use of his name. It is something only Charles Brandon and the Lady Anne use with impunity. "You must speak to me like I am your truest friend, and believe that I am your loving Thomas in return."

"Well said," Henry says. "You are the only one I can turn to, Thomas, and I must have the truth of things. What think you of Thomas Wyatt?"

"Young Thomas Wyatt?" Cromwell strokes his chin. "Why, little enough, I think. He is a useful diplomat, and serves his king very well. The only remarkable thing about him is his superficial likeness to you."

"To me?" Henry is wrong footed. "How so, Thomas?"

"Well, granted, he lacks your years of experience, but the common folk often remark on the physical likeness. Though I believe he is the shorter of the two, by an inch, he is almost as broad shouldered, and has that manly set to his jaw that so delights ladies who know you."

"Do they think him as handsome?"

"Bless me, no Henry. Those who you do not favour, and there are many these days, turn to Tom Wyatt for romantic dalliances. I believe his poetry has a certain naïve charm about it, and would appeal to foolish young girls. Perhaps they see in him, a pale reflection of you?"

"His poetry is weak, you say."

"I believe he rhymes like a lovelorn shepherd boy, and speaks of 'eyes like limpid pools', and 'breasts like twin doves'," Thomas Cromwell says, with a timely snigger. "I believe his music is almost as ... adolescent."

"That is exactly what I thought," Henry says. "I can't think why I ever believed..."

"What sire?" Cromwell asks, innocently.

"These pamphlets." Henry is embarrassed, and feels foolish that he ever doubted Lady Anne. "They say such scurrilous things."

"Against the king?" Cromwell asks. "Let me read them, and if they transgress, I will personally behead the author, and the printer."

"Ah! There is the fighting talk I so love, Thomas," Henry says. "The blood of soldiers runs in your veins."

"And yours, Henry," Thomas Cromwell reminds his king. "I still recall how you led the charge against the French, and later, when you laid out poor Charles Brandon. I swear it was the mightiest blow I have ever seen."

"I do not laugh as much, these days," Henry says. "Not since that cur, the Baron Montagu, was thrown out of court. He was a traitor … but he could make me laugh."

"I heard a funny story, but the other day, Your Majesty," Rafe Sadler says. His face does not betray how funny it is, and his lips hardly twitch. "Might I regale you with it?"

"At once, Master Sadler," Henry says. "Is it a little ribald?"

"It concerns a peacock, sire."

"A peacock?" Henry asks. "How can a peacock be funny?"

"It is not a real bird, sire, but a name given to a certain gentleman of the court. I regret that I cannot name him, for fear of causing a great scandal amongst the ladies."

"Ho, but you intrigue me, Master Rafe. Name the fellow, I command it!"

"I am sworn to secrecy, sire,"

Rafe says, "but I can drop a hint or two. This peacock fancies himself to be a poet, and a great charmer of women. He fancies himself to match his king in wit, and poetic love."

Thomas Cromwell's stomach turns over. He has just drawn Tom Wyatt back from the brink, and Rafe Sadler is bringing him back into the king's mind again. Is his protégé so angered at being left behind?

"We have business, sire," Cromwell says. "Perhaps Master Sadler might finish his tale another day?" The king's hand comes up, demanding silence, and he turns on Rafe Sadler, hovering like a hawk above its prey.

"I believe I know who your peacock is, sir, and will hear out your tale," Henry informs Cromwell's young man. "Come, out with it, for I am in a black enough mood already. Tell me of this peacock's exploits, that I might share the joke against me."

"I am told, sire, that there was once a vain peacock, well versed in the arts of poetry, and music, who fancies himself to be more handsome than Adonis."

"Does he, by God!" Henry is turning red with rage.

"One night, two beautiful women

179

set to knocking on his bedroom door."

"The swine!" Henry is shaking with anger now. "Has he no shame?"

"None, sire."

"The dog!" Henry is almost beyond rage now.

"The ladies begin to hammer at the bedroom door, and cry out," Rafe tells his enraged audience. "At last, the noise is so loud, that the peacock is forced to let them both out!"

Henry is struck dumb. Then, slowly his sides begin to quake, and he cannot contain his laughter. He begins to roar, and slaps Rafe so hard, he almost falls over. The gentlemen of the court look on, in surprise. Henry raises his arms up, wide and declares: "The peahens were trying to escape!" and continues roaring his approval. To be on the safe side, Norfolk, Suffolk, Surrey and the rest begin to laugh too.

"By God's back teeth, Thomas," Henry says, "but you have a veritable jester on your staff. See he is well treated."

"Of course, sire." Cromwell cannot believe he ever doubted his protégé, and grips Rafe's arm, to signal his approval. "In fact, there is the matter of the new Welsh advisory council. I thought Rafe might do well, amongst the heathens of Caernarfon."

"See to it." Henry is his regal self once more, and gestures, as if a movement of the finger is enough to make all things happen as they should.

"I regret, it is one of the Lord Chancellor's creations, and he might be offended if I interfere."

"The king does not interfere," Henry says. "He commands. Have it done. Is there a salary with it?"

"Forty pounds a year, sire."

"Make it fifty, but do not let Master Rafe leave my court," Henry tells him. "We need more good humoured men about the place. My dearest Cardinal Wolsey always had a ribald story, for we gentlemen. Damn, but I miss the old rascal, Thomas. Did I ever tell you how I was about to forgive him?"

"Never did a king love a subject more," Cromwell says, biting back his true feelings. "It is a poor day when Cardinal Wolsey's duties have to be spread over three lesser men. I fear poor Sir Thomas is finding things difficult, trying to decide which master he can serve, and Stephen Gardiner is little more than a competent diplomat, sire. Might I ask who was foolish enough to suggest you make him into a bishop?"

"Why, I think it was my own

idea, Thomas," Henry says, but, in truth, he cannot remember.

"Really, sire?" Cromwell shakes his head. "When I heard, I thought it was the doing of another hand. The clever, underhandedness of it, is so unlike Your Majesty's usual way of open government."

"I said you would be displeased," Henry confesses. "Then Boleyn tricked me by asking, who rules England, me or you."

"To doubt the king's right to rule this realm, is an act of treason, sire," Cromwell explains. "It is in our new laws. Which foolish Boleyn spoke thus?"

"Young George," says Henry. "We cannot have him arrested, Thomas. It will upset Lady Anne terribly. Besides, he sought only to help me."

"On the eleventh day of February, this year of Our Lord, fifteen thirty one, the great Convocation granted you the title of Singular Protector, Supreme Lord, and even, so far as the law of Christ allows, Supreme Head of the English Church, and all of its clergy. George Boleyn, Lord Rochford, was there, and helped push the legislation through. He should have known better than to interfere."

"Lady Anne was most pleased,"

Henry says. "Though I explained that it was only as far as *Christ's law allowed*."

Cromwell shakes his head. Lady Anne understands the politics of it all better than the King of England, and knows that 'as far as the law of Christ allows' is a sop to the English bishops, and means nothing in law. Whether he knows it or not, Henry is poised to become the supreme head of the church in England, and has complete power over every monastery, abbey, nunnery, and church, in the kingdom.

"Now we are stuck with a Bishop of Westminster, who cannot decide which way to jump," Cromwell replies. "With William Warham holding Canterbury, and being for the Dowager Princess..."

"Dowager?"

"She is the widow of your brother, sire. Thus, she is the Dowager Princess of Wales, and your sister, in the eyes of English law. That is why your marriage *must* be set aside. It is illegal. You must be free to marry, at your own discretion."

"Of course. What can I do?"

"Arch Bishop Warham is old, and feeble, sire," Rafe Sadler says. "He will not last out another twelve months. Then you must choose the right man to succeed."

"You must guide me in the matter, Thomas," Henry says.

"Then you must be rid of young George too."

"My God, what do you suggest?" Henry is becoming scared.

"Grant him title to several Irish estates, and put him in charge of the army over there. That will keep him from under our feet."

"An excellent solution," Henry says. It means he does not have to upset Anne, and can even make it look as if he is rewarding a member of her family. "See to it, Thomas... and do not forget to reward young Sadler. A peacock, indeed. Master Wyatt does well to be abroad, for his reputation is in tatters. We must meet with him, some time soon, and discuss his poetry. I might be able to suggest a few improvements."

"He will be most grateful, sire," Rafe replies, suppressing a smile. "For I know he is ever open to constructive criticism, from a better muse."

"Quite so, and what of poor old Warham? Who shall I appoint?"

"Fisher is a good man, sire," Cromwell says, "or perhaps my young Sadler - he might jolly things up somewhat."

"Well said, Thomas," Henry

replies. "Though his Latin might not be up to it." He laughs at his own joke, and waves them away.

They bow, and drift out of his orbit, nodding to various acquaintances, until their escape is barred by George Boleyn, who is accompanied by Sir Francis Weston, and Sir Henry Norris. They block the doorway, and seem intent on tackling Cromwell and his young man.

"Good day to you, Master Blacksmith," George Boleyn says.

"And to you, my Lord Rochford," Cromwell replies. "How goes the family millinery business? And you, Francis, were not your great relatives sheep farmers in Derbyshire? Then we have Henry Norris, whose father's father was a brewer in Norwich, and made his money running a bawdy establishment."

"That's a lie. He was an honest brewer!" Norris snaps, then realises he has only made things worse.

"You bar my way, sir." Cromwell says, and goes to push past Lord Rochford.

"Stay sir. I wish to tell you how things will be from this day forward," George Boleyn says. "I have Henry's ear, and he will appoint as I suggest. Stephen Gardiner is now Bishop of Winchester, at my request."

"A bad day's work," Rafe Sadler snaps. "You think he will support your sister, but he will not. He will set up endless committees, and groups of knowledgeable men to investigate the marriage. It will take at least five years, and your sister will be spoiled goods by then."

"Watch your tongue, Blacksmith's boy," Boleyn says, and finds a dagger pressed against his side. The speed of it, and the sheer audacity, leaves him shocked into silence.

"Now then, grandson of a hat maker," Cromwell says, "this is how it will be from this day on. Norris and Weston, you will return to your roles as panderers to the Lady Anne, and her ladies in waiting. You may even swive one or two, if the king allows it. You, Lord Rochford, will receive patents of ownership for three huge estates tomorrow. They total over fifteen thousand acres, and must be worth over eighty thousand pounds a year."

"What nonsense is this?" Boleyn cannot master his greed, and is eager to see what Cromwell proposes.

"The king wishes you to visit your new estates, at once, and take possession. He will finance the expedition to the tune of five thousand pounds."

"Expedition?" George Boleyn is confused.

"Yes, did I not mention, My Lord? The estates are in Wicklow, in Ireland, and must be subdued. I believe the current incumbent is a notorious outlaw, and rebel. Perhaps Norris and Weston might join your expedition. What say you, gentlemen?"

"I have duties in court," Norris says, at once.

"And I," Weston tells them. "I must wait on Lady Anne and her ladies, in case they need a gentleman's protection."

"Of course," Cromwell says. "Do put your knife away, Rafe. I am sure Lord Rochford wishes to tend to his packing. Good day, George, I'll see you in six months, or so. Good hunting!"

They brush the three stunned men aside, and walk through to the outer court. Several ladies curtsey, or nod their heads at the two men. To Cromwell they do it to acknowledge his position, and to Rafe Sadler, his attractiveness to them. It is known that he is Cromwell's main man, and therefore a person to attach oneself to.

*

"Master Rafe, it is good to see you again," a pretty, blonde lady says, laying her hand on his forearm. "Is there any news of your friend, Mush?"

"Alas, Lady Mary," Rafe says, "I have heard nothing. I fear it may be many more weeks before we have news."

"You do know that Mush married, just before he left England, My Lady?" Cromwell says

"I do, but men are fickle," Mary Boleyn replies. "The king is still married, yet he shares his bed with *other* ladies."

"Idle gossip," Cromwell tells her. "Do you have names?"

"I have one. I know of a dalliance of Henry's from when he was but twenty years old. Will that earn me a present of silk gloves, or a purse of gold, Master Thomas?"

"You speak in riddles," says Cromwell. "The king's affairs from his youthful years are of no concern to us, in these later days."

"The lady spoke out of bitterness," Mary says, ignoring Cromwell. "She felt as though my sister was slighting her, and, in a fit of pique, said 'I have done something that your sister has yet to do'. 'What is that', I asked, and she smiled, and said she bedded Henry years before, and made her husband a cuckold."

"This is history, madam," Rafe tells her.

"Yes, it is family history."

"Sweet Christ!" Thomas Cromwell pulls Lady Mary to one side. "Have a care, lady, for such talk might be the death of you. How sure are you of this?"

"My mother tells me that she was thirty one, and Henry somewhat younger," Mary explains. "She was visiting her great uncle, the old Duke of Norfolk, and the king came upon her, and took her aside. She claims he was inflamed with lust, and threw her dress over her head. He went to it like a bull, she claims, and accomplished the task three times, in short order. Then, he arranged for my father to stay in court, with the promise of a post abroad."

"A plausible story," Rafe says.

"Henry came to my mother's chambers each night for a full month, and stormed her, as if she were Dover castle. At last, he tired of her. The queen was at the end of a confinement, and I think he needed to sate his lust. My father is aware, but grateful for the way our family has prospered since. Once Anne opens her legs for him, Henry will have had every female in the family, and we will be related to royalty."

"It accounts for why your father received such rapid preferment," Thomas Cromwell says. "How old were you girls then?"

"Put your mind at rest, Master Cromwell. Anne was about ten, and I was two years older." Mary touches the gold crucifix at her throat. "Henry came back to the well twelve years later, and made me his new whore. A family tradition, you might say."

"It is time to find you another husband, Lady Mary," Cromwell says, "or send you down to the country. Your mother's admission is enough to ruin your sister's chances of marrying Henry."

"So, what do I care?"

"If Henry is humiliated, he will lash out. That means the end of you, your mother, and your father's career. Why, I doubt he would ever marry Anne. No, My Lady, seal your lips, and I will ensure that your mother keeps her own mouth tight closed too."

"I quite fancy a place in the country," Mary tells him. "Perhaps with a few hundred acres, and servants?"

"Lady Mary, are you trying to coerce an officer of the crown?" Cromwell says, chuckling at her effrontery.

"Of course," she replies, with a neat curtsey. "After all, I *am* a Boleyn!"

Cromwell cannot help but smile. The girl is a vixen. She lacks the refined looks of her sister, but in taking a different course, she has managed to entice a king into her bed, and seems able to ensnare any young man she wishes. He will find her some land, and a few eligible young fellows to choose from. For all he likes the girl, she will be safer up in the north, or living in a backwater of Dorset.

"Good day to you, mistress," he says. "May God seal your lovely lips, until we meet again. Lest I have to!"

10   Death in Umbria

The ochre and honey coloured Umbrian countryside rolls away into the distance, and Pippa Micheletto is touched by its almost perfect beauty. It seems hard for her to believe that it can be such a violent, and unforgiving land.

"Pippa?" The priest touches her arm, and brings her back to the present. "You must be brave. Your father would want you to stay strong, now we are close to our final intent." During the last three days, Father Geraldo has listened to her story, and become disgusted with the man she calls the condottiero.

"I'll be strong, father," she replies. "What is that town?"

"Rimini," the priest tells her. "Those must be Duke Baglioni's men." There is a column of horse, about a thousand strong, making its way towards the small sea port, with banners fluttering in the soft breeze.

"And they?" Pippa points to the horizon, where a cloud of dust denotes a second band of men. The priest shrugs. It is a time of strife, and there are columns of soldiers marching all over Umbria and, no doubt, the Veneto. Even as he shrugs, the men riding towards Rimini wheel about, and start to advance on the newcomers.

"I fear we are about to witness a confrontation, my dear," the priest mutters. "Let us stay on our little hill, and await the outcome."

"Let us pray for these newly come soldiers," Pippa says, "for surely, they must be against Baglioni. See how they spread out, as if preparing for battle. The priest un-slings the bag at his shoulder, opens it, and rummages inside. After a moment, he produces a soft leather hat, with a wide brim. He puts it on his head, and turns, so that the brim acts as a shade from the bright sunlight.

"They are pike men," Father Geraldo reports, as he squints into the distance. He slips one hand to the hilt of his concealed sword, as if to comfort himself. "There is a great cloud of dust behind them, which must mean mounted men."

"An army?" Pippa wants it to be the fabled Venetian thirty thousand, come to sweep Baglioni into the sea, but knows it cannot be. "Will they fight, Father Geraldo?"

"Perhaps they will." He frowns, and thinks. "We cannot go to Rimini, for it is held by the condottiero's men already. Perhaps we should make for these newcomers, and hope they are friends."

"Too late, I fear," Pippa says, gesturing to the two forces, who seem to have spotted one another. The troop of Baglioni's horsemen is fanning out, forming three lines. They advance on the pike men, who number but a couple of hundred, at a brisk trot.

"May God protect them, Father Geraldo says, crossing himself. "Unless God wills it otherwise, they will be engulfed."

"God cannot support Baglioni," Pippa snarls. "He cannot be so cruel."

"Hush child," the priest says. "What will be, will be. It is not for us to question His great plan."

*

"Cavalry!" Mush says, as he reigns in his mount. "About a mile off, and advancing slowly. They have seen our pike men, and mean to swallow them up, Will."

"Muskets," Will Draper calls. "Form a skirmish line behind the pike men. We have no time for ought else." With more warning, the Englishman intended to form a square, bristling with pikes, and manned, within, by musketry. "Tom, can you bring your ordinance to bear?"

"With pleasure," Tom Wyatt says, and gallops over to the two ox carts which carry his old canon. They are lashed to the beds of the carts, and his gunners are well drilled. They begin to pack the barrels with coarse grained black powder, and the new English chain shot. The poet has the carts dragged into position, on the right flank.

"Let canon roar, and muskets loose … de dah de dah…" he mutters, then decides the lines must have more work put into them on another day. His great ode to war must wait.

"Richard, join your Swiss," Will instructs. "Have them form up in two lines, a hundred abreast. Put our musketry, and the rest of the footmen behind. Mush and I will split the cavalry, and position ourselves on your flanks."

"I will do that," Richard says, hefting a pike over his shoulder. "My boys will thrust them back into yon sea."

"Hold your ranks," Mush says.

"Let yourselves be drawn out of position, and their horse will cut you down."

"Be off, pipsqueak," Richard says. "I will do my duty, if only you can do yours."

"Are there no footmen amongst the enemy?" Will asks of Mush, who has been riding ahead.

"None that I can see. I think they are little more than an advance guard," Mush says. "If their commander has any sense, he will hold off, and wait for the main army to come up. Though, God knows where they are. What would you have me do?"

"Keep to the left flank, with your two hundred riders, and hold your position, until you see me move with mine on the right. I have a mind to let them up close. They might break ranks, and attack our centre. If they do, we have a chance of winning."

"Then let us pray their general is a damned fool," Mush says, trotting off to his own, small command.

"Right lads," Richard Cromwell says, "we present arms, and hold our ground. Front rank will kneel. I want an unbroken line of steel tips, holding off their horses. Remember, no horse will ride onto pikes and spears. Hold fast, and they will be powerless." The tall Swiss sergeant at his side shouts a hurried translation for Cromwell, and the Doge's guard give a quick hurrah in return. "That's it, boys. We'll give the bastards hell!"

"And us, mate?" one of the English sailors shouts. "Do we stand here, and play with our selves?" A rough burst of laughter erupts from the crowd of seamen.

"Stay behind my pikes," Richard calls. "Can you boys throw a knife?"

"We'll take the bung out o'er a barrel at twenty paces," the sailor replies.

"Then wait until their horses stop before my pikes, and throw over my men's heads. Aim for the beasts, for the men wear steel breastplates."

"As will we, after this day!" the sailor shouts, and a great roar goes up again.

*

Father Geraldo has seen military confrontations before. In his lifetime, he has been a corn mill owner, a gentleman, and a soldier, before becoming a priest. He has fought against the French, and the Dutch in his day, and still knows how to lead a company. He can handle a sword and a spear with equal dexterity. He has killed many men, and is ashamed for it.

"Are they going to fight?" Pippa

197

asks, her heart beating in anticipation.

"Yes, I am quite sure of it, my child." The priest points away to his far right. "Baglioni's man sees only the infantry, and he means to encircle them. It must seem like an easy victory for him. Once he sees the Venetian cavalry, it will be too late to break off. If he has any sense, he will send his first and second waves right and left, to engage the enemy horse. Once they are drawn into battle, the third wave can surround the pike men, and hack them down. It will be a swift victory, if he keeps his head."

"And if he is a fool?" Pippa asks. She has a vested interest in the other side coming out victorious. As if in answer, the condottiero cavalry, led by Ando Baldini, a captain of great courage, but little imagination, spurs his mount, and charges, head on.

"He charges!" the priest shouts, and offers up a prayer of thanks. "Now all is in the melting pot."

Then the world seems to quake beneath them. Two flat bedded carts, to the right of the charging horsemen erupt in flame, and a thunderous noise shakes the heavens. Tom Wyatt's two cannon speak, and belch out their deadly loads. The priest gasps in horror, as lengths of chain, weighted at each end, fly forth, and scythe through the Perugian left flank.

The chains cut through everything in their paths, and leave a swathe of broken horses, and screaming men. Thirty or more horses are thrashing about, and a dozen men have been killed, and as many more horribly maimed. Those closest to the cannon swerve to the centre, away from the sudden carnage.

In moments, the three lines of cavalry have converged into a mass of horsemen, intent on riding down all before them. The priest shakes his head, and turns away. The battle is over, and he does not wish to watch the ensuing slaughter.

Pippa cannot turn away. She watches as Ando Baldini and his men try to storm the Swiss pike men. Horses rear up, and turn away from the twin line of steel, unable to bring themselves to close quarters. Men are unseated, and trampled underfoot, or despatched with a quick thrust of a pike, or sword. Then above the tumult, she can hear a single, loud voice, shouting in a foreign tongue.

"Rear rank, kneel!" Richard Cromwell shouts. "Kneel, you buggers. That's it. Now, muskets pick your target, and … release!" There is a sudden volley of shot, and clouds of smoke drift up into the still air. The volley is accompanied by a hail of knives, axes and wooden belaying pins. Dozens more of the condottiero's men tumble from their saddles, and the rest are starting to wheel about, and attempt a ragged retreat.

Will Draper sees that the moment is here. He draws his sword, raises it high, and urges his cavalry detachment to charge into the fray. A hundred eager Venetians raise a great cry, and spur their mounts forward. Mush sees the movement, and releases his own riders against the other flank. Though the Venetian force is outnumbered fivefold, the enemy have no wish to stay and contest the field for a moment longer.

They break, and scatter, even as Mush and Will's twin assault strikes home. The Venetians ride in, blades flashing, and exact a terrible price on their panicking opposition. Men are cut down from behind by the score. For a half hour, they ride back and forth, hacking down any man who is foolish enough to stand his ground. The Swiss pike men, who are hardened soldiers, advance in a line, and begin robbing the corpses of their fallen foes.

"These scum are mercenaries," a Swiss officer tells Richard Cromwell, with a twinkle in his eye. "They carry their wealth with them. A bag of gold or silver, a pair of fine leather riding boots, or a horse is always a welcome reward. Then there is the gold in their teeth, and earrings. As our commander, you will receive a tenth part of all the loot."

"I have missed my way in life," Richard says. "You, stop that!" One of the Swiss has found a wounded man, and is about to cut his throat. "I want prisoners. No killing of the wounded, *Tenente* Bruckner."

The big Swiss shrugs, and orders his men to take prisoners, rather than cut throats. He reassures them that the wounded can be robbed, just as easily, and reports back to his English master.

"We have a dozen wounded, and a few who have just given up," he says. "What now, sir?"

"Form a square about our musketeers, in case the condottiero army returns," Richard replies. "Then we can count the spoils. I want a full tally, which we will add to that taken by our Venetian gentlemen. Fair shares for all, eh?"

"I doubt the men will like giving up their plunder, sir."

"No? Tell them that our cavalry will have taken many horses, worth many ducats, and that they will benefit more by a collective action."

"You think like a true Swiss,

Capitano!" the man says, and goes off to spread the happy word. A horse is worth two hundred ducats, whereas a purse might only give up ten or twenty silver sou.

*

"Sound the recall," Will commands, and the young trumpeter riding by his side responds by blowing three loud blasts. All over the battlefield men reign in their mounts, and turn to answer the call from their commander. Mush is first back, at the head of a dozen of his men, and is soon followed by the rest of his command, who are shouting, and exchanging stories of personal valour. "Casualties?" Will Draper asks.

"I'll have a roll call taken," Mush replies, "though I'm sure the Swiss, and our musketeers were untouched. I'll count their dead too. About half of their men rode back to Rimini. I fear they might close the port to us."

"Master Draper, I have prisoners," Bartolommeo Rinaldi says, herding forward a young girl, and a black robed priest. "They claim to be friends, and wish to parley." Will bows to the girl, who is quite well dressed, apart from being barefoot, and then he acknowledges the tall priest.

"Forgive us, father, but we are in

the midst of a battle," he says. "Might we talk later?"

"No, my son, for we have news for you." The priest points to the walls of the nearby town. "That is not Baglioni. His main force, like yours, is elsewhere. This young lady, Donna Pippa Micheletto, has braved many hardships to reach the condottiero's enemies."

"Then we are well met," Will replies. "We will talk, but first, we must prise these fellows from under their stones."

"The good citizens of Rimini hate Malatesta Baglioni," Pippa says, quietly. "Speak to their leaders kindly, and they might well open the gates for you."

"Come with me." Will Draper beckons for a spare horse to be brought forward. "Will you ride with me to the gate?"

"I will, sir, with pleasure."

"How old are you, Donna Pippa?" Will asks as they trot down the dusty road.

"Old enough," the girl replies, warmly. "Baglioni killed my family, before my very eyes, and was intent on raping me. I escaped, and swore *vendetta* against him, and all of his bloodline, for all time."

"That is some oath," Draper

says, smiling. "Can you not simply content yourself with *his* death?"

"Perhaps … we shall see," the girl says. "Shall I act as interpreter for you?"

"Please. My Italian is not that good. Tell them that I mean no harm to the town, or its people, and wish only that they open the gates, and expel my enemies."

"Very well," Pippa tells him, and rides up to the gate. There are several prominent towns people standing on the parapet above it, waiting to hear the enemy proposals. "*Mayore,*" she begins, "This is the vanguard of a great army, sent to destroy the infamous condottiero, Malatesta Baglioni. This man is a great, and famous English soldier, in King Henry's army, and he tells me to say this to you. Cast out Baglioni's men, and surrender the city, or he will blow down your walls with his great cannon, and put everyone within to the sword. You have one hour, before he unleashes death and destruction on you all."

The mayor pales, and turns to Ando Baldini.

"Well, Signor?"

The recently defeated soldier has no answer for the man, and wishes only to escape his fate. He has lost over half his men, and doubts if the remainder will support him much longer. He looks down at the English general, and marvels at his comparative youth.

"There are ships in your harbour," he says to the mayor. "Let my men and I board them, and sail down the coast. Then you may open your gates, Signor. I shall report back to Malatesta Baglioni, for I am sure he will remember your lack of support."

"We are simple people," the mayor says. "Our city has no interest in Baglioni's plans to invade the Veneto. Now, you can warn him that a vast army is coming to destroy him." The soldier scowls, and sets off to gather his men. The mayor turns back to the Englishman, and the young girl, waiting patiently for a reply.

"Well?" Pippa asks.

"One hour, and we will open up our city to you, in friendship," the mayor shouts down. "Rimini respects, and loves the Doge, and wishes no further trouble between us. Baglioni's men will leave by sea, at once."

"A wise decision, *Mayore*," she says. "For once started, these English are like mad dogs, and cannot be called off!"

Pippa relays an inaccurate translation to Will Draper, who smiles his satisfaction. Before leaving Venice, he has agreed that the Doge's two serviceable war galleons should sail down the coast, and take station outside the harbour of Rimini, ready to support his land based expedition.

"Then they will be taken by our ships," he explains. "Once we are inside the walls, I will find you good lodgings, Donna Pippa, and you can tell me whatever you know."

*

"Father, can you say a few words over the dead?" Tom Wyatt asks the middle aged priest. "We suffered no fatalities, but theirs numbers over two hundred and fifty, and it is too warm to leave them above ground. The plague is back amongst us."

"The lenticulae, I hear," Father Geraldo replies, touching the cross hanging at his breast. "I was in Naples, five years ago, when it took hold. Almost half the city died, within two weeks."

"Then you must understand the urgency," Wyatt says. "Our English doctors think it is caused by bad air, and flies going from one corpse to another."

"Really? Modern medicine is so far advanced these days, that I am uncertain what to believe … other than in the will of Almighty God. Come, I will help lay their souls to rest, if someone else can do the digging."

"Master Cromwell's Swiss are digging a trench," Tom Wyatt explains. "It seems only fair, as they did the least of the fighting. My cannon, and the sudden horse charge seems to have won the day."

"Without the pike men, holding the line, you would have lost," the priest replies. "They were very professional, my son."

"You talk like a soldier, father, were you one?"

"Once. I served the Spanish, until I was wounded. Now I serve God. On the other hand, you do not seem very much like a mercenary," the priest says.

"God forbid! I am a diplomatic envoy and, for my sins, a poet of small worth." Tom Wyatt waves a hand at the setting sun. "I write about beauty, and love."

"Oh, a modern poet, then." Father Geraldo shakes his head at a world where a man can kill one moment, and write an ode to love the next. "I prefer the older bards."

"Who wrote in Latin or Greek," Wyatt retorts. "Poetry should be there for all the world to read."

"Perhaps you should say a few words over the dead then?"

"My verse does not translate well into Italian," Wyatt says, and smiles. "You are jesting at my expense, father."

"No, my son, just jesting." He stops, and opens the bag slung over his shoulder. From it comes a bible, and the paraphernalia of priesthood. "I hope you become more famous for your words, than your deeds, my son."

"Good day, father," Richard Cromwell says. "Come to add a little gravitas to the proceedings, I see."

"Even the departed souls of enemies must be commended to God." The priest looks the big man up and down, and sighs. "You are an unbeliever, my son."

"I believe in my great strength, and in my good friends," Richard replies.

"A great pity. God will forgive you, my son. Here, try this." The priest produces a parcel, wrapped in waxed paper.

"What is it, some holy rubbish?"

"It is a spicy, red sausage, from Apulia, and you look like a man who might appreciate it." The priest holds it out, as if in challenge.

"Will not the Bishop of Rome frown on you feeding a heretic?" Richard asks, accepting the food.

"Ah, so you are a protestant," the

priest deduces, and frowns. "The Holy Father is bishop of the entire world, my son. His title comes directly from God."

"Then God is a poor picker," Tom Wyatt says. "I met with Clement, but the other day, and find him to be … quite …"

"Human?" Father Geraldo says, and laughs. "In England, you love, and support your king, whoever he might be. There are good kings, and bad ones, just as there is the odd bad Pope. I regret that the Medici do not enhance the power of the Papal throne, but they are all we have, at the moment."

"You sound like a politician," Richard growls. Then he bites into the sausage, and his face lights up in delight. "God's teeth, but this is wonderful, father. Does it travel well?"

"They keep for years, if unopened," the priest says. "Though I doubt *you* would keep them that long."

"Not I," Richard replies. "I must show this to Will Draper, at once. His wife will find it most interesting. Imagine, Tom, our little Miriam selling this from her stalls!"

*

"I can see smoke on the horizon," Pippa says, staring from the high window of the house Will has commandeered for them.

"The Venetian ships have cannon," Will replies. "they will sink the enemy, and ensure they cannot rejoin the main forces."

"So many men killed," she says. "Drowning is not a pleasant death, I hear."

"We are at war," Will tells her. "To leave an enemy behind you, is to invite disaster. Surely, you have no love for these Perugians? Now, tell me what you know of Malatesta Baglioni."

"He is a hard, dangerous man, who can kill without a moment's hesitation," Pippa starts. "He is older than you, though not nearly as handsome, and he is armed, wherever he goes."

"I meant his dispositions," Will says, though he is pleased to be thought of as attractive by the girl. "How does he set out his men?"

"The thousand he sent to Rimini do not matter any more," says she. "My father convinced him that the Doge was going to take Rimini, and send his main army against Florence and Siena, so as to threaten Rome. He does not know that the Doge's army numbers less than a thousand men, and two miserable cannon."

"What of him?" Will presses. "Is

he with his main force?" "No, he sends Valdo, his best captain, to circle the Venetians, and cut them off from home. Then he plans to storm Venice, and sack it, before turning on Padua, and Verona." Pippa comes, and stands by Will's chair. "He is in Perugia, with less than eight hundred men. Strike at him now, and he will be caught unawares."

"It is a heaven sent opportunity," Will says, just as Pippa stoops, and puts her lips on his. He can feel her body pressing against his, and her hot mouth against him, and wants to pull her down onto his lap, and have his way with her. Instead, he gently pushes her away, and moves, so that the table is between them.

"I too am a heaven sent opportunity, Captain Will," she says.

"You are a young girl, Pippa," he says, trying to think of a better reason to refuse her generous offer. "I am far too old for you ... and ... I am married!"

"In England," she replies. "I am a virgin. Don't all men want a virgin in their beds? Take me, and make me into a woman, Englishman. Then kill Baglioni for me!"

Will starts to smile. The girl wishes to reward him for doing something he is tasked to do anyway. He thinks for a moment, then decides to sleep with his friends, next door. There is safety in numbers, he thinks, and besides, he has no wish to betray his love for Miriam.

As he takes his leave, he meets with Bartolommeo Rinaldi, who is detailed to patrol the city walls that night, with a dozen of the Swiss guards.

"Ah, Bartolommeo, the very man," Will says. "Donna Pippa is sleeping within tonight. Pray, sir, guard her well, and call on her, to ensure she is safe. Such a precious jewel must be cherished. You understand?"

The Venetian youth is flattered, and enchanted at the prospect of being so close to so pretty a young girl. He swears, on his honour to do his duty.

"Mind you do," Draper tells him, "for she is a virgin, and unsure of the ways of the world."

There, he thinks, as he goes next door, that should ensure a betrothal by morning. Donna Pippa is far to hot blooded to be left without a brave protector. By morning, Bartolommeo will be as jealous as can be, and telling everyone who will listen that he will marry the girl. Father Geraldo might even come in useful.

11   A Letter From Venice

"They call us the blacksmith's boys," Rafe Sadler says, as he stacks a pile of reports on his master's desk.

"Who do?" Cromwell asks, smiling to himself. "The children in the street, or those idlers who hang around the law courts, looking for work?"

"You know of whom I speak, master," Rafe says. He is not as thick skinned as he needs to be, Cromwell thinks. He places a soothing hand on his young assistant's back, and waves the other in the air, as if shooing away an annoying fly.

"They seek to belittle us, because they fear our strength," the Privy Councillor tells him. "Who is it who must attend the king twice a week, and who is it who fills his vacancies for him? It is I who am the prime councillor, and it is my 'blacksmith's boys' who light his fires, tend his clocks, help him dress, and wipe his arse. Am I right, Rafe?"

"Yes, master, you usually are."

"Only usually?" Cromwell puts on an alarmed look. "You mean I am wrong, now and then?"

"Never, Master Thomas, never," Rafe says. "I know they fear us, but does that not make them dangerous?"

"Only like a cornered rat," Thomas Cromwell replies. "If you wear a thick glove, one may easily screw the rat's neck. It is so with these people. They see that they are on the wrong side, and either wish to switch sides, or strike out, wildly. Apart from their insults, what else do you hear?"

"One of the Lord Chancellor's men wishes to spy for us."

"Who is it?"

"Aubrey Brierely, one of his under secretaries."

"I know him. Write to Sir Thomas, and let him know he has a traitor amongst his staff."

"He will not thank you," Rafe says. "Why must you be so fair to the man?"

"Because … because … he was a friend, once," Cromwell says. "I remember how we used to discuss politics, and exchange ideas. He was not always so stern a foe."

"He is now."

"I know." Cromwell understands, and knows that the time will soon come, when he must ease Sir Thomas More out of his office, and replace him with a cooler head. It will not be easy.

"How did your meeting with Lady Boleyn go?"

"It went," Cromwell replies. He has no intention of discussing how he was forced to bring Elizabeth Boleyn, Countess of Wiltshire, and mother of Anne and Mary, to heel. It is one thing to sleep with a young Henry, to better your family's future prospects, but quite another to boast of it, after the king has swived one of her daughters, and intends marrying a second. "She will take her secret to the grave with her."

"It is disgusting," Rafe says, with the certainty of youth. "She was more than thirty, and he, but a young fellow."

"It never happened, Rafe," Cromwell says. Rafe understands, and consigns the information to the nether regions of his mind. Her brother is the Duke of Norfolk, and she still has friends in court, so it would be foolish to goad her too far.

"I have a letter from George Boleyn. He writes, from Bristol, begging you to intercede with the king, and save him from having to go to Ireland. He swears undying friendship."

"You see? Wear a thick glove, and you shall catch your rat. I am minded to rescue him. Write to Bristol, and have him return to court. Or do you think me too forgiving, Rafe?"

"No, master." Rafe is smiling though. "Might we not write to Dublin, and bid him come home? That way, he will get the benefit of a fine sea voyage."

"An excellent idea, for a mere blacksmith's boy," Thomas Cromwell says. "See to it. Anything else?"

"A letter from Venice, sent by fast post horses, across the empire," Rafe says. "I dare say every one of Charles' agents has read it, and reported back."

"No matter." Cromwell braces himself for the news. "What does it say?"

"Nothing much." Rafe Sadler takes up the parchment, with the Doge's seal hanging from it, and reads. It is, curiously enough, written in French, so the young man does not bother to translate.

"To the esteemed, and honoured Thomas Cromwell, greetings from his dearest friend, Andrea. I wish to advise you that your embassy arrived intact, and are doing their duty, as you would wish them to."

"They are all safe then,"

Cromwell says, nodding. "Go on."

"Your poet has been away, visiting a friend in Rome, and is now with the others, performing a small duty for my city. I will write again, when things are out in the open, but for now, I can only say that your master's wish is fulfilled. The 'no' is final!"

"Excellent." Cromwell feels the need for a drink, and calls for a jug of watered wine. "Anything else?"

"Yes. Your Andrea goes on about some battle you both fought in, and mentions certain trade agreements he has concluded with our embassy."

"Trade agreements?"

"It seems that Will Draper is granted import rights for mace, black pepper corns, sausages, and Venetian wine."

"Dear God, but the man will be richer than the king!"

"I fear that it is Miriam who will prosper, master," Rafe Sadler says. "Perhaps, one day, we might look to *her* for a loan or two?"

"Why not? If the new teaching allows for women to read the bible, why cannot they be our equal in other things too?"

"I take it that the 'no' in question is what you have been waiting for?"

"It is. I must speak with Lady Anne."

"Not the king?"

"No, Anne first," Tom Cromwell replies. "For the next move is hers to make. God help her to make it well."

*

"She is in a foul mood," Lady Rochford whispers, maliciously to Cromwell, as soon as he enters the ladies chambers.

"What, not in Ireland with your beloved husband, My Lady?" Cromwell replies, smiling, graciously.

"The air will not suit me, nor the company," she replies, curtly.

"I hear strange tales about your George," he says, under his breath. "Are they true?"

"He does not lie with his lawful wife, if that is what you mean," she mutters back. "Watch out for Anne today. She is in the mood to kill."

"Ah, my dearest Lady Anne," Cromwell says, bowing low as he enters her presence. "I must thank you for granting me an audience at such short notice."

"So that I might express my displeasure at you," she snaps at him. The French lilt, used to show her affection, is gone. She sits, but pointedly does not invite the Privy Councillor to do the same. "I am furious, Cromwell, and think it is you I have to thank for my rage."

"How so, madam, when I come with the two best pieces of news any man could deliver to you. Though one is a close guarded secret, that even the king does not yet know." Cromwell holds out his hands, as if in supplication. There, I have set the trap, now walk into it, he thinks. What woman can resist knowing secrets? "Always, Cromwell is the man of great secrets," Lady Anne says, scornfully. "Do you think me so easy to placate? What have you done to my brother, you scoundrel?"

"Why, saved him, Lady Anne," Thomas Cromwell replies, innocently. "The king was furious over some poor advice he gave, and asked how best to punish him. You know what His Majesty can be like. I feared he might, in his rage, overreact."

"So, you suggest my brother be sent to Ireland?" Anne scoffs.

"I granted him lands in Ireland, that will bring him in something, one day," Cromwell says, pressing his case. "Then, once the king calmed down, I gave instructions for your brother to be recalled from Dublin."

"He is in Bristol, Cromwell," Lady Anne says. "Why have him sail to Ireland, before recalling him?"

"He must be away from court for a week or two. It will seem that he has done his penance, and will keep him safe, whilst we conduct our next piece of business. He is too outspoken, and might say the wrong thing to the king again."

"About what?"

"About my secret."

"Curse you, Cromwell." Lady Anne says, but she is calming down, and begins to suspect that something important is afoot. "I shall write to

George, and tell him to stay away from court for a month. There, will that satisfy you?"

"It will satisfy the king, Lady Anne," Thomas Cromwell replies. "Now, for my secret. May I speak to you alone?"

"H e n r y   l i k e s   m e   t o   b e accompanied, at all times," she says.

"A secret only remains a secret, without it being told too widely." Cromwell turns, and shoos Lady Rochford, Jane Seymour, and the rest from the room. Only George Boleyn's wife offers any real resistance. "Go, lady, or I will make you join your man!"

"You are a wicked old fellow," Anne Boleyn declares. "Even my mother trembles when I mention you. As if you were an old lover of hers. I say, Cromwell, you were not, were you?"

"My Lady jests. When your mother was a beauty, such as you now are, I was in Italy, cutting throats for a living."

"How delicious. Did you cut many, Master Thomas?"

"Enough, Lady Anne. Enough," Cromwell replies, smiling. She is using his first name again, and her mood is swinging. He is satisfied. "Let me whisper my secret to you, so that you might rejoice, even before the king can." Anne

Boleyn cocks her head to one side, and beckons him closer. He stands, and cannot help admire the soft swell of her breasts, and the smoothness of her neck. Had she not captured Henry, this one would have a thousand men dancing to her tune.

"The Bishop of Rome," he says softly, "has refused the annulment. I am beside myself with happiness for you."

Henry would have been dismayed, and demanded an explanation, but Anne understands at once. It is the one act that might move her closer to a crown.

"Then the break is complete?" she asks.

"He has already sent word to the Doge, and the Venetians will support him, and demand the king throws you over, or face excommunication. It could not be better for us, My Lady."

"We must tell Henry."

"In good time," Cromwell tells her. "First, we must clear the way for the news. The Lord Chancellor will, almost certainly, insist that Henry gives in to Rome, and he is a persuasive man. You must go to Henry, and tell him that you do not trust Sir Thomas, and fear he is working with the Pope. Then I will bring him the news. He will see that More has misled him, and demand his resignation."

"Give me a couple of days,"

Anne Boleyn says. "The man has crossed me once too often, and I will have his head."

"No, do not ask for that, Lady Anne," Cromwell says. If you appear too spiteful, the king might relent. He has a soft spot for More, and remembers how Cardinal Wolsey was brought down. You must ask *only* for his resignation. He will retire to Utopia, and spend his last days reading books, and dining with friends."

"He deserves to be punished."

"I say 'no'!" Cromwell's sudden change makes her jump. "It has taken me years to get to this place, Lady Anne, and you must not spoil things now."

"Must not?" She is tempted to argue with the man, but like her mother, has a certain fear of him. "Oh, very well. Have it as you wish, but if I am not queen soon…"

"We are a few weeks away from Christmas," Cromwell tells her. "Come next Christmastide, and you will be Queen of England."

"You swear?" She is suddenly like a small girl, waiting for a valued present to appear.

"I swear." Why, she does not know, but Anne turns her head, and kisses him on his cheek. He colours up, and steps back.

"You honour me too well, My Lady," he says. "Once the king dismisses More, he will want a new Lord Chancellor."

"I shall recommend you to him, of course."

"God's teeth!" Cromwell almost explodes again. "You must do nothing of the sort, Lady Anne. Advise him to ask for my candid opinion, and I will suggest a good man for the post. A man who will be manageable, and unlikely to oppose our ultimate aim."

"Then you too are heretic?" Anne says, smiling at him.

"I have read Tyndale, as have you, Lady Anne. Is it not your belief that every soul in England should be able to read an English bible?"

"It is. My hold over the king is constantly threatened by the church of Rome. We must break that hold for good," she says. "Once Henry realises that the only way forward is to take control, this country will change, for ever."

"The laws are already in place," Cromwell tells his co-conspirator. "The last Convocation made provision for the king to be head of the church in England, and my new treason laws hem the clerics in like sheep. Let them object, and I will pounce on them. We must play on the king, Lady Anne, and have him realise that he is the chosen one, anointed not by Rome, but directly by God."

"Then he will have no-one to say him nay," Anne Boleyn says. "He will dispose of Katherine, then marry me, and Rome may go and hang. Queen Anne will make a fitting partner for the king."

"Just so," Cromwell replies. "Though Katherine must not be harmed in any way. Otherwise, we will find the Holy Roman empire battering at our doors. We shall retire her, in some luxury, and let her fade, gently, away." He sees far more than Anne Boleyn can imagine, and knows that the marriage of a king is but a small part of things. Given enough time, and he shall be able to make England over, and bring justice and freedom to every citizen.

"You play a close game, Master Cromwell," Lady Anne Boleyn says. "Why do you not have Henry shower you with titles?"

"To what end, My Lady?" Cromwell asks. "I must remain a commoner, so that parliament stays on our side. I do not mind."

Nor does he. Thomas Cromwell has little time for grand titles, without power. As a common man, he will choose the next Lord Chancellor, and put in place an Arch Bishop of Canterbury. As a common man, he will bring in laws that will allow the bible to be printed in English, and he will oversee the complete subjugation of the church in England. Selling indulgences, so that the rich might buy their way out of hell, or avoid years spent in purgatory will become a thing of the past. Poor men will no longer have to pay their penny taxes to Rome, and go hungry to support rapacious abbeys, venal monks, and corrupt priests.

Give me time, Cromwell thinks, and I will help to create a brave, new order. A world that does not suffer under the threat of the Roman church. A realm that gives all men an equal chance in life.

*

"Will you dance, My Lord?" Anne Boleyn is dressed in her finest, and shines like a star up above, in Henry's eyes. He frowns, and slaps his leg, to signify that his knee, injured during the day's hunting, is hurting far too much.

"Choose a fine young fellow, and command him to partner you, my dear." Henry is a jealous man, but knows he must not entrap Anne, else she might rail against him.

"They bore me," Anne says. "I need a man, but know how to wait, my beloved one." Henry glows with pride, and gestures for her to sit beside him. She smells delightful, and is displaying her breasts in the French way, with them cinched in tightly, and thrust up towards the shoulders. The king feasts his eyes, and longs for the day she consents to his desires. He has not lain with another woman for months, and only then with her sister, Mary, who is a generous, and loving girl. Perhaps he might resort to one of the married ladies. They are usually discreet, and understand a man must relieve himself, now and then.

"They are a dreary lot tonight," Anne says. "I miss George, even though the silly boy upset you."

"Upset me?" Henry wonders where this is leading. If she demands his return to court, it will place him in a sticky position. He glances around, to see if Thomas Cromwell is nearby, and sees him leaning in an alcove, chatting with the Spanish ambassador.

"Yes, by suggesting that you make Stephen Gardiner into the Bishop of Winchester," Anne explains. "I have told him a hundred times, not to try and play at politics. He has neither the wit, nor the ability. I am just pleased you only banished him from court for a month."

"I did? I mean, why yes, it seemed the best course."

"I love your wisdom," she says,

stroking his arm. "I also wish I had your patience. Why, Sir Thomas has taken an age over the matter of the annulment. One only hopes he is playing us fair, and not influencing the Bishop of Rome against our cause."

"I trust my Lord Chancellor," Henry replies, stiffly. "He is the wisest man in all Christendom."

"Let us see," Anne says, softly. "If he is true, we will be free to marry soon. If not, I dare say the Pope will reward him well enough."

"Good God, Anne, what are you saying?" Henry's inherent mistrust begins to flare. "The man would not dare betray me!"

"But if he fails? What if he swears he did his best?"

"Then it is not good enough, and I would have his office from him!"

"Then let it be so," Anne concludes. "Pray that we soon hear from Rome. Sir Thomas is lucky that you are so benign a ruler, and would seek only his position. Perhaps a new man in the job might hurry things along."

"Not Thomas Cromwell," Henry says, quietly. "I know you like the man, and so do I, of course, but his bloodline is, well, to be frank … somewhat … diluted."

"Oh, you mean the business about him being a blacksmith's child?" Anne says. "He also tells me that, some years past, he was wont to cut throats in Italy."

"The rogue!" Henry says, admiringly.

"No, I would never suggest him for the post, but perhaps, you might consult with him. He gives much better advice than my poor dear brother, George."

"A splendid idea … should the occasion ever arise."

Henry can recall no adverse decision against a ruler, ever being given by Rome. He beckons Thomas Cromwell over, and puts the matter to him. The Privy Councillor frowns, and thinks hard. At length, he confesses his inability to remember any such case.

"The Bishop of Rome claims to be the anointed of God, and over mortal kings, and emperors. He retains their trust, and support, by allowing them indulgences. If a Pope can make your marriage legal, another can just as easily make it null and void. If Clement refuses you, sire, it is because he has been bribed, or badly advised."

"Do you mean by my Lord Chancellor?"

"Sir Thomas?" Cromwell expresses surprise. "If he fails you in any way, sire, it is in his desire to do everything he can for you. I fear he tries too hard, at too many tasks. How can a man run your realm for you, make laws, search out heretics, and deal with a corrupt, and venal Roman bishop? If anything, I would call him your greatest, and most loyal subject."

"Yes, he loves me. I know that." Henry seems relieved.

"Perhaps, it is simply that he needs a rest?" Thomas Cromwell turns away, sees Rafe hovering, then curses. "A thousand apologies, Your Majesty, but I am expecting news from my embassy to Italy, and told Master Sadler to bring it to me, no matter where I am."

"See, Anne? I have *my* blacksmith, and he has *his* saddler," Henry says, chuckling at his own, small jest. "Have him come to us. Perhaps we have good news, at long last."

Thomas Cromwell takes the refolded, and re-sealed parchment, and pulls it open with a flourish. He pretends to read, then looks up, his face a picture of horror.

"Your Majesty, Clement refuses your demands!" He crumples the missive up, as if in anger. "Sire, the Roman church have thrown down a gauntlet!"

"Then, by Christ," Henry snarls, "I shall pick it up, and dash it back at them. We must confer, my friend, and make ready our reply. For, as God is my witness, I will not settle until I have satisfaction!"

Thomas Cromwell turns to the crowded court, raises the crumpled letter above his head, and cries out: "God save Henry, King of England, and Defender of the English Church!"

The crowd roar and clap their approval. To one side, Eustace Chapuys shakes his head, and offers up a prayer for the realm, which is, in his eyes, about to turn its back on God.

*

"We must start with the monasteries," Cromwell says. "Once their revenue is ours, Henry will forget his scruples. Have our men start their enquiries at once, despite the damned weather. Let them crawl through the snow, if they must, but I want the monasteries closed, and the monks scattered."

"I will give the orders, Master Cromwell," Rafe Sadler replies. "I was thinking of putting Barnaby Fowler in charge of the task."

"Is he well enough?"

"He is recovered, sir, and ready to serve you again."

"These next few months are critical, Rafe," Cromwell says. "You understand that, don't you?"

"Of course. We must bring the church down, then re-build it in the new way," Sadler says. "Every pulpit shall have an English bible, and Rome will be erased from the realm. There will be opposition, of course. Arch Bishop Warham will speak out against the king, and Sir Thomas More will bring his power to bear against us."

"The king is smouldering," Cromwell replies. "He was for removing them both from office at once. He called poor Sir Thomas 'a wretch of unfathomable ingratitude', and swore to defrock Warham himself. I counselled otherwise."

"You are too kind, sir," Rafe tells him. "You should have them done away with."

"And made into martyrs?" Thomas Cromwell will not allow such a travesty, if he can help it. "Warham is bedridden, and will not last more than a few months. People will forget him, in time. Have him tried for treason, hanged drawn and quartered, and every catholic in England will want him made into a saint. The same goes for Sir Thomas."

"He is a wilier prospect, sir," Rafe says. "Let him, and he will do you harm."

"I told Henry that he should remove most of the Lord Chancellor's workload from his shoulders, but let him stay in office, for now. Once we start into the church, he will not be able to hold his tongue. I will condemn the abbeys, and ask him to ratify it in law."

"He will not." Rafe imagines

More's stern refusal.

"No, he will not. He will be unable to serve both Henry, and the Pope, and must choose." Cromwell can see it all, clearly. "The only way he can avoid angering the church is to refute our actions, as Lord Chancellor, and the only way he can avoid refusing the king, is to resign. He has no choice. Resign, and Henry will let him retire to Utopia. I will petition the king to let him keep his pensions, and he can live a quiet life."

"Will he do that?"

"He will." Cromwell is very sure of his man. "As long as he keeps silent, the king will not notice him. There are others who will not stay silent, and it is they we must look to."

"Norfolk?"

"No, he is more of a king's man than a catholic," Thomas Cromwell explains. "Suffolk will also be with us. I have a mind to do great things, Rafe, and must have willing men about me."

"Richard Rich is always seeking employment," Rafe Sadler replies. "Then there is Stephen Gardiner's secretary. I believe you know Master Wriothesley?"

"What, Grisley Rizley?" Cromwell shakes his head. "The man used to work for Wolsey, years ago. I put him in the way of the law, and he latched onto Stephen. I think him an ingrate, but when they sent Harry Percy to arrest my old master, I remember seeing him cry, as if grieved. Would you have him?"

"I don't trust a man who has so many masters," Rafe replies, "but he writes good law, and that is what we need."

"Very well, employ the fellow, but I don't want him hanging around Austin Friars. Understood?"

"Yes, master," Rafe says. "The house is for the inner circle, and not to be spoiled."

"Yes, exactly," Cromwell concludes. "During the coming times, we must use many varied kinds of people. Some will not match our standards, but we must tolerate them, until we reach our goal."

"Then I may take on those of the Lord Chancellor's men who feel the wind blowing against them?"

"Yes, but do not put them in positions of trust." Cromwell sighs, and wishes he had his nephew Richard, Will Draper, young Mush, and even Tom Wyatt back with him. The poet has served him well in the matter of dealing with the Bishop of Rome.

"Ambassador Chapuys is waiting to see you."

"Ah, yes. Dear Eustace must have his say. I must keep him even closer to me now," Cromwell says. "Let him come in."

Eustace Chapuys is shown in, and he bows, after removing his feathered hat. Cromwell offers him the best chair, which is always nearest the roaring fire.

"I will stand, for the moment," Chapuys says.

"Why so?" Thomas Cromwell asks." Are we then no longer friends?"

"That depends on what you are going to do with My Lady, Queen Katherine."

"The Dowager Princess Katherine, wife of the late Prince Arthur, and Princess of Wales. will receive the entitlements of her rank, Eustace. I have always held that to be so. Have I ever intimated otherwise to you? Am I now to become some monstrous creature to her?"

"The king wishes her dead," Chapuys says. "Forgive my bluntness, old friend, but fear it is so."

"The king understands that he must not offend the Emperor Charles," Cromwell explains. "Besides, I will not allow it. Within a few months, thanks to your Pope, Henry will be able to divorce himself, and marry as he wishes."

"You swear?"

"She will live in comfort."

"With her daughter?"

"Alas, not. Unless they both renounce their claim on the king, and swear themselves to the new church."

"Preposterous!"

"Eustace, my dear friend, I asked. I could do no more. Henry listens to the Boleyn woman, and she is spiteful against Henry's daughter. We do well to keep them both alive, my friend. You may visit the ladies, each once a month. I expect you to advise them as to their behaviour, and I will ensure their safety. No intricate plots, Eustace … or everyone will suffer. Henry is in the mood to hang a few Catholics, if only to flex his muscles. Have I your solemn word?" Chapuys nods, and turns to leave. "Will you not stay, and share my supper, Eustace?"

"Not tonight, Master Cromwell," the little Savoyard says. "I must resolve myself to remain your friend. These times are hard, and though you might not believe me, I wish you well. Goodnight."

"Have a care what you write to your emperor," Cromwell calls. "I am instructed to read all your correspondence. Even that which is sent via the Lombard bankers."

The ambassador stops in his tracks, and shakes his head, sadly. He has always suspected his diplomatic letters were being intercepted. Henry always seems too well informed, and able to guess his every intent.

"How long, Thomas?"

"Since you first arrived," Cromwell tells him. "Not by me, you must understand, but by the Lord Chancellor's men. It is the way of the world, Chapuys."

"No, it is the way of *this* world," he replies. "Diplomatic rules are violated, good men are destroyed, and one and a half thousand years of faith are swept aside, so that a king can put aside his lawful wife, and marry his ... whore!"

"Would you act any other way," Cromwell answers, "if your lord demanded as much?"

"What you say is true." Chapuys' shoulders slump, and he sighs. "Only I might not be quite so ardent in my duty as you, Thomas. You say that Sir Thomas More can retire, and the queen may keep her dignity, but I do not believe it. Katherine will die from a broken heart, or poison, and the Lord Chancellor will be condemned, if only out of his own mouth."

"That is for him to decide."

"No, my friend, it is already decided. Henry adopts what ever belief suits him, at the moment. He knew what you intended with your Tom Wyatt's embassy, yet plays the hurt party when the Pope falls for your shabby ruse. He is becoming a dangerous man, my friend, and I fear for us all."

The ambassador pulls on his cap, and walks out. Cromwell feels a pang of hurt, and knows that a valued friendship has been sorely damaged. Was this, he

thinks, how More and I started? He starts
after the Savoyard diplomat, as if to make
amends, but stops himself at the door.

"Friendship is the great deceiver," he mutters to himself.

"Master?" Rafe Sadler is there. Rafe is always there, ready to do his master's bidding. "What can I do for you?"

"Leave me," Cromwell says. "Find another, less ambitious man to serve, and make a new, less dangerous, path for yourself."

"I don't understand," Rafe says, though, in truth, he does.

"I am set on a certain road, and do not know if I have the strength to follow it to the end."

"Then lean on me, sir." Rafe will never abandon his master, come what may. "Let your young men be the pillars of your strength, and carry out your great work."

"Thank you, Rafe." Cromwell turns, and goes back into his warm library. "Warn our people that Ambassador Chapuys will soon set up a new way to relay news to the emperor. I am afraid I let him see how closely hemmed in we have him."

"Perhaps we might consider a plan, where we must have a new ambassador?"

"No!" Cromwell says, curtly. "Eustace Chapuys must remain in place, and unharmed. He is more than a friend to me. He is my conscience, Rafe, and I have sore need of one."

12   San Gemeni

Will Draper is desperate for a drink, but even more desperate for news of the enemy dispositions. His scouts are out, looking for the army of Malatesta Baglioni, led by his right hand man, Gino Valdo, and for the condottiero himself. He raises a wine sack to his lips, and drinks, feeling the cool watered down wine run down his throat. Perhaps it is only his imagination, but everything seems to taste sweeter, and fresher here, than back in England.

Even in November, the Umbrian countryside is as hot as England in June, and the heat of the day is slowly sapping his strength. A red faced Richard Cromwell is hiding under a tent flap, eating, as usual, whilst Tom Wyatt is scribbling away in one of his never ending series of notebooks. He is either writing a report of their progress, or ennobling them all in verse.

"Where is Mush?" Draper asks. Edward Wotton, a Cromwell spy who has joined them in the expedition, turns from the canon he is inspecting.

"He rode out at dawn," he says. "I thought you knew? He is with the Bartolommeo lad, and Wyatt's friend, Antonio Puzzi. They are restless with the inactivity, and long for battle."

"No one should want to fight," Will Draper replies. Two days before, he charged the Umbrian forces at Rimini, and killed three men. It does not make him feel good, he thinks, or add to his honour in any way. Killing is a means to an end, and if there was another way, he would take it, and sail home to his wife.

"They will scout around, and come back when they are hungry," the zoologist spy says sagely, and returns to his investigation of the two canon, which are strapped onto low ox carts. There is a slight crack in one of the barrels, and he considers what can be done about it without benefit of a gunsmith.

"She'll fire again," Tom Wyatt says, noticing Wotton's perusal of his big guns. "They did well the other day, and will do so again."

"Once, or twice, perhaps," Edward Wotton says. "Though, were it down to me, I'd set a long fuse, and stay well back, next time. Have you ever seen one of these things explode?"

"I bow to your superior knowledge," Tom Wyatt says, and returns to his poetry. The country is beautiful, and he is inspired to try out a few couplets. One day, he thinks, I must put them into a book. Off to one side some men are stirring, putting on helmets, and picking up swords and pikes. More men struggle to their feet, and reach for the nearest weapons.

"Riders," Richard tells them, stowing away the remains of a red sausage in his bag. "See the far off dust cloud? About half a dozen, I'ld guess."

Will Draper has chosen his ground well. He is camped on a low hill, and has fortified it with tangles of bush, and wooden stakes. He also has guards, with charged muskets dotted about the hilltop, and mounted men scouting the locality. He is sure the men galloping towards him now are friends, and tells Richard so.

"Tell the men to stand down," he says. A minute later, five riders come into plain sight, and ride straight for them. At closer quarters, Will recognises Mush, and then the Rinaldi boy, and some others whose names he does not recollect.

The previous evening,

Bartolommeo Rinaldi had approached him, and formally asked his permission to marry Pippa. The girl, in need of a protector, had ensnared him, after establishing his families position in Venice, and evaluating his wealth. Being related to the Doge seems to have sealed the bargain. Father Geraldo had married them, in front of a crowd of rowdy Swiss, and catcalling Venetian gallants, who always admire the romantic conquest of a beautiful girl. The climax of the evening consisted of them both being carried, bodily to the marital bed, a straw filled ox cart, and serenaded with catcalls, and lewd comments until everyone was too tired to continue.

Pippa shall make a good wife, he thinks, and Bartolommeo a most adequate provider. Will considers it to be a fine piece of work on his behalf, for having an attractive unattached girl amongst six or seven hundred men is a recipe for disaster.

Mush is galloping ahead, he reigns in sharply, and slides from the saddle, as if he were born to it. His companions are close behind, covered in fine red Umbrian dust, and beg for wine, before they collapse from the unyielding heat.

"We found them," Mush declares. "They are camped far to the

north west, making for Florence. It is as if they expect to meet the Doge's army coming at them. It will take them a day to turn about, and another two to come back, once they realise they are chasing a phantom enemy."

"You say they are camped?"

"Yes. It was early morning still, and there was little movement. It's as if they are taking all the time in the world. Perhaps they are in no rush to take on the Doge's imaginary army."

"They should have scouts pressing ahead, looking for the enemy," Will Draper says. "Once they realise there is no foe, they can wheel about, and come back on us."

"They seem perfectly content camping out where they are," Mush tells his brother -in -law.

"And what of Baglioni?" Will Draper asks.

"Bartolommeo rode to the south east," Mush tells him. "We met up, just now."

"I rode to the walls of Perugia, Signor Will," the young man reports. "It is about twelve miles distant. The town is locked up, tight, and the thick walls are manned with guards and lookouts. I asked the sentry at the main gate if I might enter, but was refused. He had orders to turn everyone away. Then, as I turned to leave, a officer came to the wall, and shouted down for me to wait a moment. He asked me where I came from."

"What did you tell him?" Will asks.

"That I was coming from Siena, where I saw a vast army. I told him it was marching down south, towards Rome."

"The man asked me what else I knew, so I told him that Rimini had fallen to another great Venetian army, and that it was going on from there, to help in the sack of Rome."

"I bet that stirred them up."

"It did. The man demanded to know how I knew so much, and I told him that soldiers were also coming down from Lombardy, and up from Puglia to join in the storming of Rome. The officer grew more friendly then, and said they had changed their minds, and that I could enter the town, but I said not, and that I would ride on to Rome, where the Pope was to be deposed by the Doge, and there was to be a great battle. He shouted down for the guards on the gate to detain me, but I rode off, as if on the road to Rome. Did I do well, Signor?"

"Well enough, my friend," Will Draper says. "Malatesta Baglioni now knows Rimini is taken, and his forces there are destroyed. He has two choices now. He can either stay inside the walls of his Perugian fortress, and hope we do not have enough cannon to make his walls fall down, or he can take his men to Rome, and meet up with his main force. If Rome stands squarely behind him, he will have a formidable force … and no-one to fight."

"Then we might catch him on the road," Tom Wyatt says.

"Why not let him get to Rome, and have the Venetian army attack him?" Richard Cromwell asks.

"We *are* the Venetian army, Richard," Mush reminds him. "You must stay out of the heat more often, my friend. Baglioni will find out he has been tricked, and head north to join his own *real* army. Once that happens, we are lost. He will invade the Veneto, take Padua, then lay siege to the city and destroy Venice's power, for ever."

"Sorry, I wasn't thinking straight," Richard says, wiping his brow. "So, how do we stop him?"

"It depends on which path he chooses. If he stays in Perugia, we are powerless," Will tells them. "If he makes a run for Rome, we can cut the road, and force him to fight."

"Are we strong enough?" Tom

Wyatt is well aware that their little army has a hard core of Swiss pike men, surrounded by a few hundred enthusiastic amateurs. They have won one battle, but riding down fleeing men is hardly going to make them into seasoned troops.

"My Swiss will stand," Richard says.

"Are you doubting our horsemen?" Mush asks. "They charged into the enemy well enough the other day."

"This is different," Will Draper confesses. "Malatesta Baglioni is a survivor. He will have kept back his best men, and they will be well armed, with muskets, and lances. Rather than charge us, he will spread his force out, and probe for our weakest parts."

"We have the canon." Edward Wotton says. He bends down, and uses his finger to draw in the red dust. "Put them here, in the centre, and make a show of putting our best troops around them."

"Then strengthen our wings?" Will asks. It is a sound enough idea, but one a wily opponent might expect. "I doubt Baglioni will fall for it, Master Wotton. If I were him, facing a larger force, I would find a favourable place to make a stand. A narrowing of the road, between two hills, perhaps."

"There are such places," Bartolommeo Rinaldi says. He too sketches in the Umbrian dust. "Her is Perugia, and here, Rome. The hills at this point, narrow. There is a small walled village, called San Gemini. The fortifications are very old, early Roman, and it sits astride the Via Flaminia."

"What's that?" Richard asks.

"The road that runs through the town is two thousand years old, and was built by the ancient Romans," Bartolommeo explains to the big Englishman. "They built the town as an outpost, back then, and threw up a circle of walls. Later they built a second, outer wall. You could hold the outer walls with a hundred men, and there is a slope, up to some old ruins, a legion's winter camp, I believe."

"That is where he will make for," Will says. "He'll send men ahead to secure San Gemini. Then he'll bring the main force on, once he knows he is unopposed. If we are not there to challenge him, he will ride for Rome."

"And if we are?" Wotton mutters, ill at ease.

"We stop him there," Draper says, firmly. "We block his path, and fight."

"It is almost forty miles to San Gemeni," Tom Wyatt says. "If he starts right away, he will have a fifteen mile start on us. We will never get there first."

"Not all of us," Will Draper replies. He can see the coming battle in his mind's eye, and understands what must be done. "I want about thirty men, Mush. They must be the best we have, well armed, and all able riders."

"You mean to ride for San Gemini, without the support of our cannon, and foot soldiers?" Edward Wotton asks. He is a cautious man, and seeks for a safer way forward. "What if Malatesta Baglioni gets there first? He'll cut any advance guard to pieces, and still take the village."

"Then we must ride like the furies," Will says. "Mush, select your men, quickly. We leave in half an hour."

251

"You intend leading this mad dash?" Tom Wyatt says. "I must find myself a swifter mount."

"No, Tom," Will tells him. "You must remain in command of the main body. Keep both foot, and horse together, and advance on the village. If Richard can keep his Swiss marching, you will arrive half a day behind us."

"I'll make the buggers run, if need be, Will," Richard Cromwell boasts. "They may not understand a decent language, but they fight like Englishmen. Besides, my sailors will set the pace."

"Then we will meet at San Gemini, tomorrow, my friends," Will Draper says, walking towards his horse. "Come on fast, and hard at them, Tom. Don't let our boys see how tough the enemy look. Just push the Swiss forward, and hit them from right and left with the cavalry."

"I will do as you say," Thomas Wyatt replies, clasping his friend's hand in farewell. "Though I doubt the coming fight will be as easy as the last. I fear we will lose many good men."

"There is no other way," Will tells him. "If Baglioni survives, and rejoins his army, Venice is lost."

"God's speed to you all," the poet calls, as Mush rides up with almost three dozen mounted men. Will Draper recognises a few faces amongst the volunteers, but Tom Wyatt singles out one face from the crowd.

"Sir, I know you, do I not?"

"Capitano Giovanni Ipolatto, at your service, Signor Wyatt," the man says, bowing in the saddle. "You did me a small service, by delivering a purse of silver to my wife and family, in Venice."

"Then, sir, you should stand down," Tom Wyatt replies. "This is not the sort of wild thing a married man with two small children should be undertaking. Tell him, Will. Let only single men go on your mad caper!"

"What say you, Capitano Ipolatto?" Mush asks. "We are off on a dangerous bit of business. Think of your wife."

"And yours, sir … and yours, Signor Mush?" the Venetian retorts. "Or Bartolommeo Rinaldi, who I see amongst us? Do not dishonour us by making us stay behind."

"There is your answer, Tom," Will Draper says. "Let each man know his own desires. Now, we ride!"

Tom Wyatt watches the small party gallop off. If they make it to San Gemini before Baglioni, they will have to bar the gates, and hold the walls for at least half a day. He must follow at speed, despite half his men being on foot. He is cursing their lack of fresh horses when, a thought comes to him, and he turns to seek out the English zoologist, and part time spy, Edward Wotton.

"Master Wotton, remove the cannon from their carts, and spike them. Then, you will fill the empty carts with as many Swiss pike men as you can. Next, you must assign any men still on foot, to a horseman, so that they might double up in the saddle," he commands. "In this way, we might raise our speed from three miles each hour to four, or even five."

"The horses will go lame under the added weight," Edward Wotton advises. "They will be useless when it comes to the charge."

"Then we charge on foot," the poet replies, sharply. "A line of pike men to the fore, and the rest behind. Once the sides meet, we will not need horses … just the nerve to stand, and fight!"

"Come, child, let me find you a place on one of the ox carts," Father Geraldo tells the young girl left in his charge. "Your scant weight will make no difference."

"No, father, I will keep apace on foot. As you will be doing," Pippa says. "For I sense you wish to be there, come the reckoning."

"You are an astute young lady," the priest replies.

"Astute enough to know that you were not simply wandering about the countryside." Donna Pippa likes the priest and, though she knows he has been lying to her since they met, she has, until now, been willing to accept his half truths. "You speak Italian well, but like a foreigner. You choose an Italian name, but are more likely French, or Spanish."

"Am I?"

"Walking to Venice, indeed. Your shoes are remarkably under worn for that to be the case. You forget, my father was a spy for the Doge, and I am my father's daughter, sir. I don't know what is behind the cross, father, but I can trust you, and am content to stay with you."

"I am … or rather was, a soldier," the priest replies. He wonders why he has kept his mission secret, even now, when he is amongst friends.

"I guessed that by the way you fought those villains the other day," says Pippa. "I guessed that you became too old for soldiering, and became a priest."

"Something along those lines," the priest admits. "I was badly wounded, fighting in Spain. As you rightly thought, I am not Italian. I almost died from my wounds, but I had a vision, and it saved me."

"A holy vision?" Pippa is awe struck. In a society where religion, and devotion to the church is everything, a visitation from above is something to make your heart beat faster.

"Our Lady came to me, and touched my brow. My wounds healed, as if by her will." The priest touches a finger tip to the spot, and sighs. "I knew then, that my life must be given to God, and set about taking holy orders. Once I was a true son of God, I wanted to do more. I want to gather together men who have the strength of character to become soldiers of Christ. Not for temporal armies, you understand, but for God. I want an army to serve God in the darkest places of this world, where evil still reigns."

"You scare me, father," Pippa says, and she shudders. "Is that what you were about … looking for … soldiers?"

"I was going to seek out those with a like desire." The priest raises the cross at his neck, and kisses it. "My name is Ignatius of Loyola. My voices tell me to visit Venice, Milan, and Paris, where I shall find like minded men, ready to sacrifice their all for the kingdom of Christ Our Lord. When I have the beginnings of God's great, evangelical army, Our Lady commands me to go to Rome, and offer ourselves to the Pope."

"He is a Medici," Pippa says. "He worships gold, not God."

"He is God's instrument," Father Ignatius says. "When the time comes, Our Lady will guide me."

"Amen," says Pippa. "In the meantime, may she guide us to San Gemini in time."

"Oh, we will get there in time," the priest says, "and the Mother of Christ will watch over us. I have seen it."

"You know the future?" Pippa asks. She is spellbound, and believes every word the priest utters. After all, he has been touched by God.

"I am not a magician," Father Ignatius Loyola tells her. "I am only shown that which concerns me. I will gather my holy soldiers, and march on Rome, where the Pope will welcome me, and recognise my true purpose. He will send me forth, with my soldiers, to do good works in His name."

"I must find you a halo, father," Tom Wyatt says, as he trots up, alongside the priest, and the spellbound young girl. "Does your God command you to fight with us tomorrow?"

"He does not," Father Ignatius replies. "It is my own wish to join you. I believe my mission in life is to seek out darkness, and fill it with light. Malatesta Baglioni is part of that darkness."

"Then take a place on one of the carts, or behind one of the outriders," the poet says. "Donna Pippa, you may ride behind me, if you wish."

"If Father Ignatius will consent to ride in the cart, I will accept your offer, sir." Pippa gives a cheeky little curtsey, and raises a foot to the proffered stirrup. "Though we might get on better if I take the reigns, and you hold on to me."

"God's teeth," Wyatt mutters, as her soft, warm body nuzzles into his back. "Bartolommeo has his hands full with you!"

*

The priest walks beside one of the carts. He is now forty years old, but as fit as any man in the company. His leg wound never seems to worry him, whilst he is about God's work, and in going to destroy Malatesta Baglioni, that is what he is doing.

"Bless me, father," one of the Swiss says. The priest smiles at him, and raises his hand in blessing. Two more men jump from the cart, and force him to climb aboard. "Your presence will lend wings to our wheels, father," the first man explains, and they all laugh.

"I am blessed in falling in with such a company," Ignatius Loyola replies, hurriedly blessing the entire retinue. "We are on God's work, my sons."

"And when it is done, we will be about our own," one of the Swiss says. "The condottiero's men will all have their wealth with them!"

"Let us not dwell on these earthly things, my children," Father Ignatius tells them. "Though I must remind you all that, if I fight tomorrow, it is as God's own mercenary ... and he will expect to receive his just reward."

"Well spoken, father," one of the Swiss captains replies. "Our commander says that we shall all have equal shares. With luck, you might end up being the richest priest in Umbria."

"What profit's a man with gold, if he loses his immortal soul, my son?" Ignatius says, and lays a hand on the man's arm. The grizzled Swiss soldier cannot take his eyes away from the priest's, and he crosses himself.

"Father, if I am spared tomorrow, I will put off my armour, and follow you. Will you have me?"

"Can you renounce all worldly goods, and walk in the valley of the shadow, my son?" Father Ignatius asks. "If so, then you shall be the first soldier in my company of Christ."

The rest of the cart's passengers cross themselves, convinced they are in the presence of something beyond human understanding.

"Don't steal away too many of my men just yet, priest," Richard Cromwell calls from the next cart. "After the fighting is done, you may have all of the bastards, with my blessing!"

13   The Medici

Alessandro Medici cannot help but be angry at the messenger who, still dirt stained from the road, is grovelling at his feet. He recalls from his school days, that in ancient times, those who bring bad news were often executed, and he is sorely tempted to have the terrified man taken out, and beheaded.

Instead, the almost twenty year old, newly installed ruler of Florence, gives the man a swift kick in the ribs. He is still a youth, but his tall, muscular build, coupled with his suspiciously dark skin tone, makes him a feared potentate. As the next Duke of Florence, he promises to be a strong, but harsh ruler.

"How many are they?" he demands of the man, who can only shrug his lack of knowledge.

"They filled the sky line, sire," he says, for wont of anything better to say. "A man might spend a week counting them."

"How far off are they?" the duke demands.

"A day's march." The man sees a chink of light. "They did not seem to be heading straight for the city, My Lord."

"Your Magnificence?"

"Pardon, sire?"

"I am to be addressed as Your Magnificence, or Serene Highness," Alessandro Medici informs him.

"A thousand pardons, Your Serene, and Magnificent Majesty."

"Oh, I like that one," the duke replies, softening his stern stance. "Yes, that sounds quite splendid, Giuseppe, and to think, I was going to have you killed!"

"I thank you for your kindness in sparing me, Your Eminence."

"Not Eminence," Alessandro says. Though it is a closely guarded family secret, Alessandro Medici is, in fact the illegitimate son of Giulio Medici, and an attractive African serving girl. As his father is now Pope Clement, it might be disrespectful for him to purloin one of his own favoured titles. "You say this army is not coming here?"

"I cannot say for a sureness, My Lord … Magnificence… but they have camped out across the high road to Verona. Perhaps that is their intended destination?"

"Perhaps," the duke mutters. He is not party to his father's various machinations, and wonders if this is part of one of his schemes. The Pope, who he visits rarely, is not the usual sort of father figure, and often invites him to orgies, where vast quantities of wine and women are consumed.

Alessandro Medici does not suffer from the same vices, and prefers to stay with the same mistress. Donna Taddea Malaspina is a beautiful courtesan, who has sworn to remain faithful to him. This eliminates any chance of catching the dreaded French disease, or one of the lesser forms of sexual malady.

Just that morning he has received a long, rambling letter from Pope Clement, in which his natural father talks about some obscure English legal matter, his new mistress, and a thinly disguised hint that he is about to arrange a magnificent marriage for him, to a French princess.

This, the astute Alessandro knows, is one of his father's worst ideas to date. He recalls that it was his father who allowed the Florentines to establish a republic in the city, and throw the Medici family out, and that it was only Emperor Charles, his army, and the traitor, Malatesta Baglioni, who restored the status quo.

Charles will not tolerate a marriage into the French royal family, even if the girl is illegitimate. Only two years earlier, the emperor and Pope Clement had made an informal deal to marry Alessandro off to one of his own illegitimate daughters.

One hint that this new marriage is to take place, and an army of Spanish and German mercenaries would appear at his gates, to put a stop to it. No, he must write, and decline the offer from his befuddled father, whilst making the Holy Roman Emperor, Charles V aware that he is still a good catch for little Margaret.

The emperor has several illegitimate children, and marriage to one of them, Margaret, aged seven, will bind the Medici clan to the Holy Roman Emperor, the most powerful man in the world. The union must proceed without hindrance, the duke realises. He calls for a scribe, and begins to dictate an urgent reply to his father.

It is clear to him that Clement has accepted something in return for the marriage into the French royal house, and wonders what kind of a mess his father has created. He hopes that it is only a matter of a bribe, which can be repaid, and not something dangerous. Then he remembers the muddled paragraph about

England, and he decides to re-read the letter.

After a second perusal of the document, he groans to himself. His father, Pope Clement, supreme head of the church, is giving King Henry the perfect excuse to rip apart the Papacy. The young duke can see what will happen, and realises that with a protestant England, northern Europe in a turmoil of religious reform, and dangerous Lutheran doctrines flying about, the map of Europe will change forever.

"Your Magnificence?" The messenger who has brought news of an unknown army asks. "Have you any further need of me?"

"Yes, I have, Giuseppe," Alessandro, Duke of Florence replies. "You must have them bring you a fresh horse, and prepare to ride to Rome, at once."

"Yes, Majesty." The young man hesitates. "May I ask why?"

"An urgent message for the Pope."

"Oh."

"What in God's burning Hell does that mean?" Alessandro demands. "You sound as if I am asking you to ride to the moon!"

"No, sire, but if the message is important…"

"Spit it out man."

"It's just that … His Holiness swore at me the last time I tried to deliver a letter from you, and uttered profanities. Then he made me wait, in an ante room, for three days and nights. Finally, he took the letter, called you a filthy word, and tossed it aside, without even breaking the seal. Why will the same not happen again?"

The Pope, in his declining years, has come to mistrust everyone, including his own illegitimate son, and suspects intrigues in every missive. Alessandro understands, and makes light of being called 'an ungrateful bastard', and '*Il Moro*', a reference to his African blood, but this French nonsense must be stopped, at once.

"Have them saddle up two horses, and inform my bodyguard that we ride for Rome, this very morning."

"But, Your Highness," Giuseppe says. "You have only been back in power for as few months. Is it wise leaving the city?"

"Have the sons of the mayor, and his council arrested," the new duke says. "Any trouble, and they are to be flayed alive, then impaled on the city walls."

"An excellent solution, Your …"

"Oh, cut out all the titles, I'm getting bored with them. From now on, 'sire', and 'my lord' will suffice. And you can stop kneeling every time you are in my presence. A few grovelling bows will do, for now."

"Too kind, My Lord," Giuseppe replies, climbing to his feet, but still managing to put in a deep bow. "I shall have the hostages collected at once, and arrange for the bodyguard to assemble."

"Not all of them," the duke says. "Perhaps fifty, or sixty will suffice."

*

It takes a couple of hours, but Alessandro Medici, Duke of Florence is on the road for a face to face meeting with his father, Pope Clement. His bodyguard, bedecked in the latest steel breastplates, and with visored helmets, and armed with either an arquebus, or steel tipped lances, ride close behind, three abreast, and fifteen deep.

The going is quite easy, thanks to the old Roman Clodia Way, which will take them to their destination, without having to ride through rough terrain. The cobbles beneath their feet are sixteen hundred years old, and the sound of horses hooves makes it sound like an army on the march.

With such men at his back, the duke feels safe enough, and knows that no robber band will be foolish enough to try their hand with him. He is contemplating riding on, through the night, with reed and tar torches to light the way, when he sees the first soldiers, marching ahead. They are on foot, and seem ill disciplined.

"Giuseppe," he says, turning to his herald. "Gallop on ahead, and enquire of those soldiers, as to their destination, and from whence they came."

"Yes, sire." He hesitates, then plucks up the courage to ask a pertinent question. "What if they kill me, sire?"

"Then I will know their intentions," Alessandro replies. "Rest easy, my friend. My guard will avenge your murder, ten fold."

"Thank you, sire," Giuseppe says, and spurs his horse on, after the straddle of men ahead. As he draws near, they turn about, and one or two hold up their pikes, in a warning manner. Another one steps forward, hand on the hilt of his sword.

"Stay, sir. What do you want of us?"

"Nothing, my good fellows, but to enquire who you might be, and where you might be heading." Giuseppe concludes this speech by taking the wineskin from his pommel, and offering the dozen men a draught of wine. "Hand it around, my friends, I have more, back with my company. The threat is much understated, but he draws their attention to the sixty, heavily armed cavalry, a bare five hundred paces away. One glance tells the men on foot to accept the wine, and hold their peace.

"As to who we are, sir," their spokesman says, "we are but a few common soldiers, late of the army of Malatesta Baglioni, under the command of his general, Gino Valdo."

"Then the army near Florence is the condottiero's?"

"Yes, sir. We camped, resting up, before the final push, on to Verona. Then we were to take Padua. I dare say, when old Baglioni arrives, he'll end up looting Venice."

"Happy news, fellow," Giuseppe tells him. "Here, take my purse for your trouble." He throws across a purse of silver. Enough, he calculates to buy them a bed for the night, and a couple of cheaper whores to hand around. "Why are you fellows on the road to Rome though?"

"A scouting party, sir." The man waves a hand at the dozen or so strapping, well armed fellows in his company. "We heard rumours that Pope Clement's army was close, and have been sent to meet them, and lead them back to our base."

"S p l e n d i d !" G i u s e p p e announces. "Clement's army, together with Malatesta Baglioni, will sweep aside all our foes. My master will be delighted with your news, and wish to join in the final kill. I must go, and tell him these tidings, at once."

Giuseppe cannot believe his luck. Such news will astound the duke, and he will be well rewarded. The wine, and the few silver coins were well invested. He spurs his horse hard, and gallops back to where his master is waiting, impatiently. Once he hears the news, he will wish to join up with Baglioni's army, and ensure he gets a cut of the spoils.

*

"*Cozza*," the soldiers spokesman says, and spits on the ground. "Come on lads, let's get a move on, before they realise we are deserters."

"Scouting ahead, that was a good one, Umberto," a second man says, and laughs. "Do you really think they'll ride to the camp?"

"Like a well aimed arrow," Umberto says. "Once that mincing little *finocchio* tells his lord what I've said, the stuck up *stronzo* will be off, at the gallop!"

"And good luck to them," another tells them.

"Let the bastards rot," Umberto replies. "Tell them something they don't want to know, and they'd have ridden us into the road."

*

"Well?" the duke asks, the moment Giuseppe is in earshot.

"It is the condottiero's men," the herald calls out. "They are scouts, but the army I saw near Florence, belongs to the traitor, Malatesta Baglioni!"

"Great God, but this is a lucky day for me," Alessandro Medici says. "My father can go hang!"

"His Holiness is said to be coming on, at the head of a great host," Giuseppe reports. "He means to destroy the Doge, once and for all, by the sound of it."

"And cut me out of the deal?" the duke snaps. "Curse him, and damn his soul, for we will join Baglioni."

"Just being at the scene will entitle you to a share of the spoils, sire," Giuseppe says.

"Well done, my faithful friend," Alessandro Medici tells his herald. "For this day's work, I will reward you well. With two armies, and our own troops, we will be able to take Siena on the way, then Verona and Padua will fall. Imagine it, half of Italy in our hands."

"Do we return to Florence, and raise our levy, sire?"

"No, we ride to Malatesta Baglioni's camp, and make ourselves known."

"Baglioni isn't with them, sire."

"No, then *Il Moro* will take command, until he comes."

"Forgive my forwardness, sire, but the name suits you, both in temperament, and power."

"Yes, it does, doesn't it?" The Medici duke seems, suddenly, to accept his ill starred birth, and welcomes recognition of his black bloodline. Let them call him '*Il Moro*' if they wish. For proud Moorish blood runs in his veins. His mother, a Medici serving girl, called Simonetta da Collevecchio is a tall, ebony skinned woman, still only in her late thirties, who lives quietly in Florence now, with servants of her own. "We ride, men, to Venice, and to glory!"

There is a ragged cheer as his bodyguard sense the possibility of pillage, with little personal danger, and an exciting few weeks away from the dullness of Florence.

*

"We need to be here," Malatesta Baglioni says, stabbing the point of his dagger at Rome on his wall map. "If Valdo is marching there, we must join him."

"Why would he, sir?" one of his captain's asks. "His orders are to advance towards Venice, and encircle the Doge's army."

"He must have heard that Rimini has fallen," Baglioni tells him. "He realises that the Venetians might get between him and the Pope's forces, and is falling back on the city. We cannot be left, stranded in Perugia."

"The walls are thick, and we have almost six hundred men, sir," the same man persists. "We can withstand a six month siege."

"To what end?" Baglioni shakes his head, vigorously. "No, we ride to Rome, and I take command of our army. The Venetians cannot stand against me, but I *must* reach Rome."

"We have horses enough for all, sir," another officer says. "We can take the Via Flaminia, and be there inside two days. If only the enemy do not think to cut the road."

"Where would they attempt such a thing?" Baglioni asks. The man pores over the map, then points.

"There. San Gemini is a fortified hill village, straddling the road," he explains. "Even a small force, occupying the place, might stop us."

"Then we must reach there first," Baglioni decides. "Pick fifty of my best men, and send them off now. We will follow on, once we are ready."

"What about the camp women, sir?" the first officer asks. "Some of the men have taken town girls, and will want them along."

"No."

"They will insist," another officer says, unwisely.

"Will they, by God?" Malatesta Baglioni's mouth is like a cruel slash across his face. "Tell the men of my decision. Whichever of them complains first, and will not move without his woman, is to be bound, and made to watch the whore be handed around the rest. Then you will hang her, and ask who else wishes to complain."

"Yes, sir." The officer's voice is sullen, as he has a woman who he wishes to keep with him, but he goes off to obey his master. The condottieri live by a common vow, and each man is bound by strict rules of etiquette, and loyalty. To betray one's comrades means the end, for you, and all of your family.

"Will these dogs never learn?" Baglioni snaps to the remaining officers. "I help bring down Florence, and make them all well off. Then I take Perugia, and they are given land, and any woman they wish to take. Next, I will give them the freedom of Venice. All I ask is that they obey, and fight like demons."

"Every man in your army will fight to the death for you, condottiero," one says, and the others murmur their approval. To be a mercenary in the army of Malatesta Baglioni is to be part of one of the truly elite fighting forces in the world, and no man would have it otherwise.

"Then send out the advance party, and let the rest of us prepare," Baglioni concludes. "For, by tomorrow, I intend being in Rome, or dead, with a sword in my hand!"

*

Alessandro Medici does not think it unusual when his small party are not challenged by the camp's guards, nor is he unduly worried that no-one rushes forward to offer their greetings. It is the heat of the day, and most of the men are in one of the three thousand tents littering the plain. It is only when they gallop into the roughly formed square, at the epicentre of the mercenary army's camp that he notices the unnatural quiet.

"Giuseppe, dismount and roust a guard of honour. Don't these dogs recognise royalty when they see it?"

The herald stays on his horse. He can see men lying inside some of the nearest tents, and some others are wandering about in the near distance, as if unsure of what to do. Then, a lone man emerges from the nearest tent, holding his hands up, as if in supplication.

"Sweet Jesus!" Giuseppe cries in horror, wheeling his horse about. "It is the plague ... the *lenticulae* are on his face already. Ride, sire, ride for your life!"

The bodyguard are already milling about, trying to turn, and gallop away from the horror. The Medici duke gasps in horror, and holds a scarf to his mouth. Then Giuseppe catches his reigns, and leads him away from the carnage of invisible death.

Gino Valdo has pitched his camp there, because his men are becoming weak with the sweats. By the second day, they are bed bound, or suffering fits and hallucinations. Now, the lentulae are appearing on their skins, and they are moving into the agonising final hours.

Apart from a few hundred, who desert and flee at the first sign of sickness, the entire army is now affected. By tomorrow, five thousand will be dead, and by the next day, ten or twelve thousand shall have succumbed. After seven days, it will have run its course, and Malatesta Baglioni's army will be a memory. Two thirds of them will be dead, and the remainder nothing more than shadows of their former selves. The bones of over fourteen thousand men will lie in the hot sun for months, until some brave souls gather them for burial, and steal the silver from their purses.

Alessandro Medici, Duke of

Florence, rides back to his city at full gallop, and shuts himself away in his palazzo. His ever faithful Giuseppe gives orders to close the gates to everyone, and issues instructions for the populace to stay indoors, and ration their food, until further notice. Medici cowers in his bed, made impotent by the thought of plague. The idea that he might be tainted by it will stay with him for days, until he fails to become sick, but the fear will haunt him for the rest of his short, violent life.

*

Guido Monticelli's mount is beginning to blow under him, and he realises the horse will not last another mile. He is in charge of Malatesta Baglioni's spearhead, and is sworn to reach San Gemini, before the enemy can block their way. Behind him, are fifty of the hardest men in Italy, all determined to gain the walls of the fortified village, and hold them, come what may.

Monticelli slows to a canter, and is about to dismount, when they reach a small crest, and look down. In the distance, they can see San Gemini. The mercenary leader forgets his ailing horse, and kicks it into a gallop. One last rush, and the village is at their mercy.

"*Fottuta Cristo!*" The shocking blasphemy erupts from the man to

Monticelli's left. He curses again, and points at a group of dots, moving across the valley bottom. Their leader understands at once, and urges his men on. He is outpaced by those with sounder mounts, and they race for the village, knowing they must arrive first.

The enemy, about thirty in number, also spur their horses forward, and a madcap chase ensues, as each side rides for the village's single, wooden gate. It is standing open, and unguarded in the late midday heat, and beckons both sides on, invitingly. Baglioni's man screams for his men to hurry, but sees that the Venetian force has a small lead.

*

Will Draper is hunched over his saddle, urging his horse on to one last effort. All about him, his men's mounts are beginning to pant, and stumble. Mush, the slightest amongst them goads his horse into the lead, and then, in the blink of an eye, he is through the gate, and leaping to the ground, sword already in hand.

As more of the Venetians gain the safety of the inner wall, Mush is already starting to shout out orders. Will Draper dismounts, and looks about for those of his men with muskets. He grabs one, and shouts for the rest to follow. He urges his man up onto the low wall, and tells the others to man the parapet, and prepare to offer shot to the enemy.

He is convinced that Baglioni's men will dismount, and spread out, ready to lay siege, but he is wrong. Monticelli's men ride at the gate, full tilt, with spears couched, as if they will force their way in with sheer bravado. Tom Wyatt's friend, Antonio Puzzi, and Bartolommeo Rinaldi, are each pushing one side of the gate shut, even as the leading riders arrive, and lunge at the rapidly narrowing entrance.

Puzzi cannot avoid one of the sudden spear thrusts. He takes the point of one in his left shoulder, but continues to push as if his life depends on it. Other men are running up, and lending their weight to the task. After a frantic few moments, the gates are closed, and a bar slid across. A sword is thrust through the small grating in the gate, as if to try and skewer anyone still by the door. Mush knocks it aside, and thrusts his own blade out. There is a sudden scream, and a volley of curses.

Will Draper is pulling his musketeers into a rough line, and urges them to take aim. Heavy barrels rest on the fortification's thick Roman wall, and a dozen men crouch, to look for a near enough target. Then they discharge their muskets in a ragged volley. A great cloud of gunpowder smoke billows up into the air, and the men rash enough to still be pounding at the gate take the full effect.

They curse, and tumble back, out of range, leaving behind four dead. Will's men send up a cheer, and begin the laborious task of reloading their muskets. Each stage must be meticulously completed, else the gun might fail to discharge, or even blow up in their faces.

"Hold fast, lads," Will Draper says. "They are out of our range now. If they venture near, give fire to them again." He jumps from the parapet, and seeks out Mush, who is standing with Bartolommeo. "Fine work at the gate, my friend. Is Antonio badly hurt?"

"The spear went in barely an inch," the young Venetian replies, "but it has torn his shoulder muscle. He can still hold a sword. What now?"

"It will take their leader some time to think about his options," Draper tells them. "Then he will realise how little time he has to take this place. I doubt he has enough men to storm the walls in different places, simultaneously, so he must settle for the gate."

"Some of them have muskets, and I saw some arquebusiers amongst them," Mush says. "Perhaps they might try and shoot us from the walls?"

"If it were I," says Will Draper, "Then I'd concentrate all my guns opposite the gate, and keep firing at it, and the walls on each side. Then, whilst we are keeping our heads down, out of sight, they could charge the gate with a battering ram."

"L i k e   t h e   R o m a n s ? " Bartolommeo rubs his chin. "They will need a very stout tree trunk, and at least fifty men to batter away with. They are too few, Will."

"All they need is a cart from the fields," Will explains. If they fill it with heavy stones, it will be a formidable ram. If the man has enough wits, he might command them to pack it with straw too. Then, soak it in lamp oil, set fire to it, and use horses to draw it close. A few dedicated men at the back, pushing, and the job is done."

"Surely, the gate will hold?" Bartolommeo asks.

"Probably, but it will be weakened, and the flames will take hold and do even more damage. Then, under cover of the attack, by no more than a dozen men, I would have the main force rush to an unguarded part of the outer wall, and scale it with ladders. Once on the wall, we will have the devils own job driving them off."

"Then let us hope our adversary is stupid," Mush says, smiling. "In the meantime, do we stay together, or man the entire wall?"

"Signor, whose men are you?" A timid, round bellied man, in his fifties, approaches from one of the nearby tumble of white painted houses.

"We are the Venetian army," Mush replies, gesturing to the thirty odd men awaiting orders. "And you, sir?"

"I am the mayor. We feared you were the condottiero's men again. Each time they come, they rob us, and take which ever girls they want. How can we help?"

"How many able men have you?"

"Within the walls?" the mayor thinks for a moment. "Perhaps sixty, but we are not soldiers, signor."

"Call them together, and tell them to bring anything they can use as a weapon. Sharpened staves, or a billhook lashed to a long pole will do. Have them stand at the walls, five paces apart, and look as soldierly as they can." Will knows such men have little military value, but if they are above the enemy, and alongside a fighting man, they might stand their ground. "Mush, have your men position

283

themselves between each villager, so as to give them strength. Then, will you keep a close eye on our musketeers?"

"I shall, Will," Mush replies. "With a hundred men, we can cover almost all of the outer wall."

"You must be ready with your musketeers, Mush, to rush to any part where we are hard pressed."

"We have about four hours of good light left," Mush replies. "Do you think they will risk fighting in the dark?"

"They might," Will says. In truth, he has no idea how the condottiero's men with handle themselves. Stumbling about in the dark, carrying a wooden ladder might not be to their taste. Most mercenaries will fight well, but only if they know they have a decent chance of success. "We must hold out until nightfall, then be doubly on our guard. Let the men sleep in shifts, so the wall always looks well manned."

"When do you think Tom Wyatt will arrive?" Mush asks.

"After the main body of Malatesta Baglioni," Will tells his friend. "The condottiero will want to storm our walls, and take the village. Then he can assess the strength coming against him, and make his plans. I doubt that even Richard Cromwell's Swiss pike men can stand against volley fire from their arquebusiers. Once their formation is broken, Baglioni will open the gates, and rush out with his mounted spearmen."

"Then we lose?"

"By then, if it comes to pass," Will says, "we will be already dead, and no longer concerned."

"We were outnumbered by the Welsh rebels," Mush says, firmly, "and we won. Before that, you served the king abroad, and cut your way through the enemy Irish."

"Wild eyed men with axes, and hunting bows," Will says.

"Hunting bows?" The mayor has been listening, trying to pick out what these Englishmen are saying. His own English is poor, but he catches these two words. In painstaking English, he says: "We have hunting bows in the village, Signor. It is for ... how is it to say ... hunting the *belve*?"

"Wild beasts?" Mush considers. "They have hunting bows, Will. Sixty men who can bring a deer down, on the run, at a hundred paces." Draper smiles, and begins to think that things are beginning to shift their way.

"Perhaps," he says, "Father Ignatius' prayers are beginning to work!"

14   The Siege

Despite having fought his way from the toe of Italy, up to Milan, and back to Perugia, and also being a favoured captain in Malatesta Baglioni's mercenary army, Guido Monticelli is more of a soldier than a tactician. He sits on his horse, out of musket range, and ponders what his master would do.

At length, he decides that Baglioni would storm the walls, with ladders, and battering rams, or blow down the gates with his canon, and put everyone to the sword. Now, he thinks, how do I do this, without a canon, no ladders, and only fifty odd men.

"Marco," he says to his lieutenant, "I need ladders."

"We can lash the boughs of trees together," Marco replies. "I will set some of the men to the task."

"Good. I also need a canon."

"Alas," Marco says, shrugging. "For that we must send to Perugia. It will take three or four days."

"Then I must have a battering ram," the captain tells his friend. "How do we do this?"

"A wagon," the younger man replies. "We can load it with kindling wood, and set it on fire, once we ram it into the gate."

"My thoughts, exactly, Marco," his captain tells him. "See to it, at once. I want to be in the village before nightfall."

"Shall I put a sack of gunpowder in the wagon?" Marco asks, warming to his task. "We don't have enough to blow the gate open, but it will make a splendid flash, and frighten the defenders. I assume we will use the wagon as a diversion, and storm the walls further around, with the ladders?"

"You read my mind, Marco," Monticelli says, nodding his approval. "But time is of the essence."

*

"There is a wagon coming," Giovanni Ipolatto calls from his place on the wall. He is flanked by two surly looking villagers with hunting bows at the ready. There are sixty archers dotted around the wall, waiting to defend their village.

Will Draper joins him, and watches as the heavy vehicle is pushed into position. He sees that some enterprising soldier has nailed planks of wood to the cart, so that they stick out at right angles, and provide cover for the pushers. One of the villagers, a big, square jawed peasant, casually draws his bow, and sends an arrow on its way. The shaft hits one of the defensive planks, and buries itself in the wood.

"Pray, save your arrows," Will says, in his halting Italian. "Wait until you can see them clearly." The man grunts, and lowers his bow.

"They mean to fire the wagon, and run it into the gate," Antonio Puzzi says. "How do we stop them?"

"We do not," Will explains. "It is a ruse. Even if the fire takes hold, it will take an hour for it to burn through the gate. Our foe means us to mass at the gate, and wait for them to batter their way in. Then, he will come around one side or another, and try to climb onto the parapet, using ladders."

"Where?" Mush shouts up. He has a dozen musketeers with him, and wishes to know where they can do the most good. Will does not know. The main attack could come at any part of the old Roman wall.

"Hold fast, Mush," he shouts down. "I'll gather together a few men with bows, and see if we can get them to the right place."

There is sudden arquebus fire. A few armed men, hiding behind the advancing wagon have chanced firing off a volley. The man who had loosed off an arrow earlier, sees a glimpse of flesh, and aims. The arrow hits one of the attackers in an exposed elbow, and he screams in pain.

The defenders cheer, and a few more arrows wing their way to the wagon, where they embed themselves in wood. The wagon is feet away from the gate, and an arm appears, holding a blazing torch. A villager reacts like the hunter he

289

is, and puts an arrow into the arm. The man staggers back, and two more arrows slam into him. As he falls, another mercenary snatches up the torch, and tosses it into the wagon, just before another arrow takes him in the throat.

The villagers are finding their courage, and a dozen arrows pepper the attackers wagon. The firebrand catches the hay in the cart, and it flares up. The heavy cart thuds into the gate, and the sack of gunpowder ignites, sending a tongue of flame and smoke into the still air.

The men immediately above the gate leap for their lives, and one of the villagers is engulfed in fire. More men run towards the gate, and start to throw stones, and arrows into the conflagration. The dozen men who have pushed the wagon turn, and run for their lives. Several villagers send a steady stream of arrows after them, and three are brought down.

Will Draper knows he cannot wait any longer. The main attack must come from either the scrubland to his right, or the old remains on the nearby hill, and he must choose. He considers for a moment, then waves towards the stretch of wall to his left. It is guarded by six of his own men, and a dozen villagers.

"There, Mush," he cries, and as he does, forty men rush from the ruins, carrying a half dozen ladders, crude things made from lashed together tree branches, and race for the sparsely defended stretch of wall.

Mush and his men arrive, just as the enemy are throwing up the first ladders. His men gain the parapet, even as the first attackers appear. Some manage to discharge their muskets, and one of the men on the ladders screams and falls back. Then more ladders are there, and men are coming over the wall, yelling in fury, and ready to kill.

Will arrives as the villagers start to back away. He grabs one of them, and orders him to draw his bow. The man does so, and sends his arrow into the chest of a big man who is waving an axe. The others rally, and from a few yards away, begin to loose off arrows. The attack seems to be wavering, when another ladder is up, and Monticelli is first over. He throws himself into the gaggle of villagers, and cuts two of them down. The rest jump for their lives, or run away.

Monticelli realises how poorly defended the walls are, and rushes at Mush's musketeers. Will Draper steps in front of them, sword in hand, and takes the first rush. The mercenary is over confident, and Will parries his blade, and puts in a quick riposte. The big man knocks Will's blade aside with the dagger in his left hand, and steps back.

More men are gaining the wall, and Will must act. He feints at his opponent, and encourages him into another lunge. The Englishman evades the lunge, and flicks his sword point across Monticelli's unguarded face. The tip rips open the man's cheek. He cries out, and cuts, trying to catch Will across the side, but he is too slow. Will avoids the clumsy stroke, half turns on the narrow parapet, and drives his blade home. It rips through the mercenary's leather jerkin, and pierces the heart.

As Monticelli topples from the parapet, Mush darts past Will, drives his sword into another attacker, and throws himself at the ladder. He heaves, and it does not move. Then others are alongside him, and the ladder is dislodged. It topples back, throwing two men to the ground.

Will is already hacking away at another of the attackers, who falls back under the onslaught. From a safe distance, the villagers take heart, and begin to rain arrows at those who have gained the parapet. Three more men are struck with arrows, and others begin to back away, towards the ladders. Then, as if a cloud has burst, the enemy are cascading over the wall, and running away. Several of the musketeers aim, and bring down fleeing men, and the villagers, sensing an unexpected victory return to the walls, and shower the mercenaries with arrows.

It is over, and has taken no more than ten or fifteen minutes. To the defenders on the wall, it seems as though they have been fighting for hours, and they are utterly exhausted. Will goes from man to man, and congratulates them for standing firm. Mush moves from body to body, and collects their purses and silver crosses on fine chains.

"A God fearing bunch of men," he tells Will, holding up the religious charms. "Perhaps Father Ignatius' prayers were stronger."

Giovanni Ipolatto bends over the man he killed, and searches for his hidden purse. Then he compares boots, and decides the dead man's are grander, and of the right size. Antonio Puzzi, more of a diplomat than a soldier disapproves, but will accept his share later.

"That was a close run thing," Bartolommeo Rinaldi says, as he joins them. "We drove them off at the portal, and the villagers are putting out the fire. We have saved the gate, Signor."

"Did you lose any men?"

"No. Though one villager was scorched. And you?"

"Five of our men, and six villagers," Will tells him. "I count seven of their men dead inside the walls, and another eight or nine as they ran away."

"We killed four of them at the gate," the young Venetian says, proudly. "That makes about twenty dead for their part. Is it enough?"

"Perhaps," Will replies. "They might decide to wait for the rest of their army. If what we hear is right, Baglioni will arrive with about four or five hundred men. If they get here first, we will be dead before noon."

"But we stood them off," Bartolommeo says, with a hurt tone in his voice. He is young, and does not want to hear that he might ever lose.

"Sixty men," Will explains. "Tomorrow, they will come from all sides. We cannot defend the entire wall. As soon as Baglioni takes the outer wall, the villagers will melt away, and pray for salvation. We will have to fight odds of twelve to one."

"Is that all," Mush says. "Then they best go carefully!"

*

Marco Spolletto cannot believe

that the attack has failed, or that his friend, and commanding officer is dead. He considers what can be done, with a third of his men already thrown away on an ill omened attack. His men, he thinks. The condottiero will hold him responsible, what ever happens now. Unless the Venetians surrender, he has no chance of dislodging them before Baglioni arrives at first light.

"Hey, Marco," one of the men asks, "what now?"

"Ride up to the wall, and ask if they want to give up," he says, sarcastically. To his utter surprise, the short, barrel-chested man, known to his comrades as *La Talpa* ... the Mole, jumps into the saddle, and gallops off. He stops by the gate, and after a brief conversation with one of the Venetian defenders, rides back.

"Well, what did they say?" Marco asks.

"*Fottiti*," the Mole replies, and his comrades roar with laughter. Why not, they think. The Venetians are safe inside, and they must spend a cold night in the open air, waiting for the morning. So, telling the enemy to go and *fottiti* is an apt response.

"Why don't we wait until dark, creep up, and slip over the wall. They

295

can't watch every bit of it." This comes from Dandino, one of the younger men.

"No, but if we are discovered, they will just beat out our brains as we climb over," Marco says. "Hands up anyone who wants to try?" Not a hand moves. They are professional fighting men, not lunatics. The consensus of opinion is that they bed down, and wait for help.

*

"They are unsaddling," Mush reports to Will Draper. "I think they've had enough for now."

"Thank God," Will says. "I doubt we'd be able to stand off another charge. Some of the younger men are beginning to understand about mortality."

"And you?" Mush asks. "You seem more cautious, these days."

"You must blame your sister for that," Will replies. Miriam has changed his outlook on life, and he wants nothing more than to live to a ripe old age with her. "Do you not think about Gwen?"

"Not whilst I am killing," the olive skinned young man explains. "I seem able to put her out of my mind in moments of great danger."

"Would that I could," Will says. He imagines what she has been about, this remarkable wife of his, and wonders how her business affairs are progressing. With her earnings, his own small fortune, and what he hopes to gain from his Italian sojourn, they should be able to buy the house they currently lease, along with the land to the right and left.

River frontage is becoming popular with the newly enriched, or ennobled, so that they might keep a barge, or a small skiff. With such a craft it makes crossing from north to south of the great river so much easier, and allows for the better flow of news from the southern ports.

Information, Thomas Cromwell says, is power, and must be gathered in like a rich corn harvest. Miriam Draper cares little for the political life, and wants more land, and another boat, so that she might start to grow her own produce, and open new market stalls throughout Kent, Surrey, and Sussex. Added to the promises of the Venetian Doge, the future seems bright.

All that is left to do is to survive the next day.

*

"Let any man who falters be abandoned," Malatesta Baglioni commands. "We must make San Gemini by dawn. If Monticelli has the fortress, he will need relief, and if the fool has failed me, we must take the place before the Venetian army arrives."

"As you wish, My Lord," Ando Frascallo replies. "With this moon, we should be able to ride deep into the night."

There is the sudden, urgent beat of horses hooves, coming from ahead. The riders, uncaring of the growing gloom, are desperate to reach their master with the latest news. Baglioni reigns in, and waits for the three scouts to gallop up to him.

"What news?" Frascallo calls.

"The best, sir!" one of the men replies. "I came on the Venetian army, not three hours ago. They number less than six hundred, and are coming on in carts, like invalids."

"No horse?" Baglioni asks.

"Yes, but they are riding two to a beast," the second scout informs his master. "The Frenchman reached San Gemini."

"Tell me the worst," the condottiero snaps, and the French mercenary scowls at his companion.

"I arrived just after the Venetians had repelled our men," he confesses. "San Gemini is in their hands, and our boys have taken a beating."

"God's eyes, but I'll skin

Monticelli," the condottiero curses.

"He is dead," the Frenchman replies. "Killed on the battlements, I was told."

"You spoke to our men?"

"Marco is in charge," the French mercenary explains. "He has enough men to bottle them up inside, but fears the Venetians coming up behind him."

"How far away are they?" Baglioni knows he must reach the fortified village first, and take it, if he is to defeat the enemy. Once beaten, they will scatter, and the road to Rome will be open. He is yet to hear that Pope Clement has renounced him, and that his army is dying, day by day, outside Florence's walls.

"A few miles further off than us," the first scout replies. "If we keep up a steady pace, we will arrive hours before they do."

"Then we must keep on," Baglioni decides. "Ando, send twenty men on ahead, at the gallop. Tell them to join up with Marco, and keep the Venetians locked inside San Gemini. Have Marco's men set themselves to firing at the walls, all night. I want the bastards inside to be tired out by dawn!"

*

Mush is enjoying himself. The

Perugians outside the wall have started to fire off their arquebus' at various intervals, to keep everyone awake, so he is giving them something to aim at. With several of the village boys, he devises a clever ploy to help turn the tables on his foes.

In pairs, Mush has his men spread out along the wall, one with an arrow already knocked in his bow, and the other with a wooden stave with a hat, or helmet on it. The game, though a dangerous one, is keeping them amused, and frustrating the enemy gunners.

One village lad crouches, and moves his raised stave back and forth. The Perugian gunner sees the movement, and discharges his arquebus. The second villager, watches for the flash, and swiftly looses off a couple of arrows at it. After a half dozen exchanges, there is a scream from the dark, and the guns cease to fire.

"Good shooting," Mush says to the lad, and drops a couple of silver coins into his hand. "These Perugians squeal like pigs, my friend."

"Bastards," the youth replies. "They raped my sister, the last time they came to us."

"Never again," Mush says, scowling into the dark. "Tomorrow, we will kill them. How many of your people will fight with us?"

"Ten or twelve," the village boy tells Mush. "The young ones, like us, and a couple of the older men. The Borsini brothers are fine hunters, and hate the condottiero's men even more than we."

An hour before dawn, Will Draper is on the parapet, watching the arrival of more enemy horsemen. They number about twenty, and are the vanguard of the condottiero's army. He wonders how long his own small force can last, without Tom Wyatt and the rest of the Venetians.

He is still there, as dawn breaks. One of the women from the village is making her way along the ramparts with a basket, from which she hands out hunks of hard bread. A second, younger, girl follows, with a wine skin. There is a ragged cheer from the besiegers, as they see a welcome sight.

The army of the condottiero appears in the distance, and comes on at a goodly pace. Will shouts orders, and his tired men take their places on the wall. They are armed with a mixture of bows, muskets and, with little else to hand, piles of stones to use as missiles.

Will Draper knows that a concerted rush by two or three hundred men will be enough to take San Gemini. The stones and arrows might thin down the enemy a little, but ultimately, it is going to be down to hand to hand fighting. At the far end of the parapet, he sees Mush waving, and gesturing to the north west, where a sizeable dust cloud has appeared.

It is the Venetians. Using carts, loaded with men, and horses carrying two, Tom Wyatt has gained several hours, and is almost within striking distance. Even as Will sees them, they are noticed by Malatesta Baglioni, who issues orders for his plan of battle. Will can only watch, as the Perugian force splits into columns, and prepares for battle.

"What are they doing?" Mush asks, as he comes running up to his friend. He has only ever seen skirmishes, where two lines of men hack at one another, until one side breaks. Now, a squadron of Baglioni's horsemen have turned about, and are cantering away from the field of operations.

"This condottiero knows his business," Will Draper explains. "He knows he is slightly outnumbered, and seeks to even out the odds. See how he is positioning his spearmen? They will form a line on foot, to face our pike men, and hold them."

"Why?"

"He seeks to lure our young gallants out from behind the screen of Swiss, and draw them back towards the village. When they come on to him, his horse will fall on their flank, and break them."

"Tom Wyatt will not let that happen," Mush says.

"He will not be able to hold them back, if they sense victory," Draper replies, knowingly. "Once they break, he will sweep around the Swiss flank, and force them into a square. After that, the end will come quickly."

"What can we do?"

"Hope Tom can keep his young heroes in check," Will says, "or hope Baglioni's men make a mistake we can exploit."

"Will they?" Mush asks, and his friend shrugs.

*

"Single line abreast," Richard Cromwell commands, as his well drilled Swiss pike men tumble from their carts. "Pikes forward sloped, and advance at a slow march." His orders are translated, and pass from man to man. They are amongst the best trained mercenaries in Europe, and will keep the line firm.

"Fall in, behind the pikes," Tom

Wyatt shouts, and his crowd of young Venetian gentlemen spread across the narrow valley mouth, eager to be at the enemy. "Hold back, until I give the … oh, damn!"

A group of thirty or forty of his men spill around the line of pikes, and start to advance on the right flank. Wyatt sees the danger, but cannot bring them back under control. More follow, and soon, two thirds of the Venetian force are advancing on the Perugians, like an undisciplined mob.

Baglioni smiles, and orders his spearmen forward, to stop the Swiss advance. The two lines face one another, and trade insults across five paces of no man's land. Then he gives the word, and his arquebus men spread out, behind the spearmen, and begin to pick off the Swiss.

Tom Wyatt, seeing he cannot hold his men, runs forward with them, screaming, and waving his sword. They are less than fifty paces away from Baglioni's seemingly unprotected left, when his horsemen reappear, and storm into Wyatt's disarrayed force. For a brief moment the young Venetians look as if they might withstand the charge, but once the Perugian foot soldiers join in, they begin to back away, seeking the safety of higher ground.

Mush watches in disbelief, as his comrades start to fall. They step back, defending themselves all the way, but are taking heavy losses. He cannot understand why he is not taking part in the wild mêlée, and turns to Will for orders.

"I want every man willing to fight here, beside me on the wall. Fetch the Perugian ladders we took yesterday." Mush goes off to carry out his friend's commands, wondering how they can turn about the onrushing disaster. On the parapet, Will waits, and prays for their luck to change.

The Swiss are standing their ground, despite losing a dozen men to arquebus fire, and Richard is pacing up and down behind them, urging them to stand firm. He does not know how it will end, but he shall not be the first to break.

Tom Wyatt's men are in full flight now, making for the Roman ruins on the nearby hill, with half of Baglioni's force pressing home their advantage. It is then that Will Draper's hopes are realised. The sixty besiegers outside the gate can see that victory is theirs, and want to be in on the kill, if only to ensure their share of the spoils. They give a great shout, and rush after their comrades.

"Ladders down!" Will helps lower the ladders down to the red earth, and leads his men down them. He has about twenty five well armed men, and a dozen of the villagers, armed with bows, and axes. "Into them lads, and let there be no quarter given."

The small force storm into the unsuspecting arquebusiers, and cut them down from behind, before plunging into the line of Perugian spearmen. The attack is so savage, and from so unexpected a direction that twenty men die before they realise the danger. Richard Cromwell sees, and orders his men to charge. The entire line of spearmen crumbles away,

"To the hill!" Will Draper, his sword red with blood, yells, and sets off after the fleeing Venetians. His men, the villagers, and a swarm of Swiss pike men surge after him, and smash into the Perugian rear. Their horsemen turn, and unable to face the deadly pike thrusts, ride for their lives. Tom Wyatt rallies his young men, and throws them into a swift counter attack.

From total defeat, comes total victory. The Perugians who cannot escape, throw down their arms, and surrender. Will calls for them to be taken captive, but many are cut down, despite being unarmed. At last, the four Englishmen manage to regain control of their men, and have them round up prisoners.

Malatesta Baglioni is astounded by the sudden turnabout in his fortunes, and curses the men who deserted their posts at the walled village. Had they stayed in place, the day was his. Now he must flee. He turns his horse from the disaster, and spurs it into a full gallop.

One of the villagers sees the action, and looses off an arrow at the fleeing Perugian. The shaft catches the horse in the withers, and the beast crashes down, in a flailing mass of legs, and cursing soldier. Baglioni staggers to his feet, but a dozen men are surrounding him, with drawn swords. He nods, and, drawing his own blade, throws it to the ground.

"I beg for quarter," he says. "I am Malatesta Baglioni, Lord of Perugia, and I am under the protection of His Holiness, Pope Clement!"

"I am Thomas Wyatt, emissary from the court of King Henry of England, Signor, and I have some bad news for you. The Pope has withdrawn his favour, and declared himself against your invasion of Venice."

"A pity, Englishman, but that will not stop my army from taking Padua and Verona. It must be at the gates of the city, even as we speak."

"No, sir, it is camped outside Florence, when last we heard, and hardly stirring. I fear your army has fallen asleep, My Lord."

Malatesta Baglioni shrugs. There is always another way out of disaster, and he will emerge from this present difficulty, and return even stronger.

"Sir, I thank you for this news, now … pray, take me to your leader!"

15   Vendetta

"How goes it, Richard?" Will Draper asks. In the final rush, he has taken a stab to the side. It is a minor injury, but his friends insist he stays in the quarters provided by the grateful villagers.

"A hard won fight, my friend,"

Richard Cromwell replies. "I thought we were lost, until you appeared, like a demented spirit of retribution. Even the priest was looking worried. Donna Pippa took up a short sword, and was ready to kill any man who broke her part of the line."

"An amazing girl," Will says. "How did her husband fare?"

"Bartolommeo is unharmed, though we did lose a goodly lot of fine men. Antonio Puzzi was killed, just as their line broke, and that Ipolatto fellow, who Tom wished to stay behind, was cut down by one of their horsemen."

"Tom knew his wife, I believe. We must ensure his widow receives his share of the spoils. What of the rest?"

"I lost twenty of my Swiss. Wyatt's boys lost the most heavily. About sixty of them dead, and as many more wounded," Richard replies. "The Doge will have much to mourn. Apart from you, and Mush, only seven of those holding the village still live, and two of them are under Father Ignatius Loyola's care. He hovers over them, waiting to help their souls into heaven."

"He is a remarkable man, for a priest," Will says.

"Indeed. He blessed every one of my Swiss, and took up a pike, when a gap appeared. He fought like a real soldier."

"Then he too must have his share," says Will. "What of the Perugians? I think many must have escaped."

"Those on horseback, yes," Richard Cromwell explains. "Of those that stood their ground, we killed over two hundred, and took a hundred more prisoner. They will not raise much in ransom, but their purses were as fat as those of their dead friends. Tom Wyatt tells me that the booty comes to a little over six thousand ducats."

"So much?"

"Mercenaries like to carry their fortunes with them," Richard replies. "Each man will receive nine gold ducats a piece."

"Now I must deal with this troublesome condottiero," Draper tells his friend. "Though I wish he had been gentleman enough to die in battle. I am loath to hang a man, just for being a good soldier."

"*Cozza!*" Donna Pippa's anger seems out of place in such a slight, pretty young thing. "He murders my family, and wishes to rape me. He is the devil!" She puts down a pewter tray filled with fresh fruit, bread, and cheese. "There. I hope he chokes on it. Now, I will bring you wine.

Red, or white?"

"White," Richard Cromwell says. "It is the more refreshing. That girl is a ..."

"Witch?" Will concludes. "But such a pretty one. Fetch this Malatesta Baglioni to me."

Richard steps outside, and returns, a moment later with the condottiero, bound with ropes. He thrusts the man into a chair, and turns to leave.

"The ropes, Richard, please?" Will Draper is sure he can handle the man, who looks nothing like he has imagined. Perhaps, he might make a grab for the fruit knife, and give him an excuse to kill him. The Doge will be unhappy that the man lives. Richard Cromwell mutters, but cuts the man's bonds.

Pippa returns with a second tray, bearing two goblets, and a flask each of the local red and white wines. She pours a measure of the white, and hands it to Will. Then she goes as if to leave.

"And my guest too," Will tells her. The girl must look the man in the eyes, and come to terms with her burning hatred. It is time to stop this ridiculous *vendetta*, once and for all time. Pippa looks set to refuse, or argue, but relents. She picks up one of the flasks, and fills a second cup. Baglioni takes it from her, and grins at her nervousness.

"Ah, the sweet little girl from Perugia," he says. "When you ran away, I was forced to execute some of the towns people, as a warning. Your replacement also paid, with her life."

"Pig!" Pippa raises the flask, but Will's warning look stalls her actions. Instead, she puts it down, and retires from the room.

"What am I going to do with you?" Will muses. Baglioni raises his wine, as if toasting his foe, and drains the goblet.

"You might call your whore back, and have her stoke the fire for me. My feet are cold. Then you might as well release me."

"How can you think I will do that?" Will has the power of the Doge behind him, but recalls being warned that Venice cannot be an active player.

"Andrea Gritti will disown your actions, and make noises about having you arrested," Baglioni says. "Then he will put you on a ship, and send you home. Clement will not dare do anything either. I know too much, and can make life very uncomfortable for them both. You must either murder me, at once, or let me go. You are an Englishman, and I do not think you can kill in cold blood."

"You were about to invade Venice."

"Was I?" Baglioni smiles. "I sent my army to Florence, on manoeuvres. The duke is a Medici ally, and invited me. Now, I am told, my army is camped near the city, offering violence to no one."

"The Doge of Venice...."

"Is a practical man," the condottiero says, finishing the sentence. "The threat to Venice is no more, and he wishes to remain friends with the emperor. No, I regret that you are in a quandary, my friend."

"You have murdered people."

"I am a ruler. Does not your king have people killed?" The warlord grins. "I dare say he has killed a hundred fold more than I. As for your whore's family ... they were all spies. Now, will you kill me, or release me? I can be back inside Perugia inside the day, where I'll lick my wounds, and wait for an easier foe. May I ask the name of the only man ever to best me in a fight?"

"Captain Will Draper, sir, though not at your service," Will says, hating what he must do. "Very well, get out."

The condottiero stays in his seat. He stares at the Englishman in disbelief.

"What have you done?"

"Done? I'm setting you free."

"You bastard!" the condottiero spits, angrily. "I would rather die with a sword in my hand, than this."

"Are you mad?" Will Draper is nonplussed. The man is sitting very still, slowly clenching, and unclenching his right fist.

"No, not mad," Pippa says. She comes into the room, picks up the flask of red wine, and pours the dregs onto the stone floor. "A little tired, perhaps, condottiero?"

"Bitch!" he cries. "It was you?"

"Just so. I am the bitch who swore *vendetta* against you, Malatesta Baglioni." Pippa crosses to the last unoccupied seat, and sits down to wait. "First, your feet grow cold. Then they become numb, and the sensation slowly creeps up your body. Once I knew which flask Signor Will would drink from, it was easy to put the hemlock in the other."

"Hemlock?" Will Draper is beginning to understand, but is powerless against so cunning a young woman. "You mean the poison?"

"Yes, I distilled it days ago, for just such an opportunity," Pippa explains. "Had we lost today, I would have swallowed it, rather than let Baglioni and his dogs have me. It is a slow acting potion, that makes your body go asleep,

314

inch by inch."

"Is there an antidote?"

"Would I tell you, if there were?" Pippa smiles. "There, my dear Malatesta, you can scarcely move now. Soon, your throat will seize up, and you will choke to death, in silent agony."

The condottiero tries to stand, but his body barely moves, and he slumps sideways, gurgling.

"Dear Christ!" Will Draper is horrified, and cannot believe how coldly Donna Pippa is behaving.

"Hear the noise?" she asks, innocently. "That is his throat closing, and his last breath is being choked off. His eyes will flicker for a few minutes more, until his mind ceases to work. His last thought will be that I, a mere girl, have caused his destruction."

"Dear God, what is this?" Father Ignatius Loyola is in the doorway. He takes in the scene, and crosses to the dying man. He tries to open his lips, then feels for a pulse.

"Hemlock," Pippa explains.

"A slow, cold sort of a death for so hot blooded a man, my son," Father Ignatius says, closing the man's eye lids for the last time. Like many priests, he has some medical knowledge, and is quite aware of the deadly effects of hemlock.

So, he admits temporal defeat, and begins to administer the last rites to Malatesta Baglioni, the last, great, condottiero.

*

Richard Cromwell is sad to be leaving Venice behind, for truth to tell, it has been the happiest time of his young life to date, and the food, the wine, and the open, happy go lucky people suit his temperament well. He knows his uncle will be pleased with their success, and see that they are all well rewarded, but he doubts any amount of gold will make up for the warmth, and friendliness of the Italian people.

"Apart from them trying to kill us … twice," Mush tells his friend.

"It was nothing personal," Richard responds. "Malatesta Baglioni would have had to fight anyone who came against him. It was his nature."

"To think, it took a girl to bring him down." Mush shrugs, and continues packing.

*

"Our fastest galley will transport you to Marseilles," Andrea Gritti explains. "From there, post horses are waiting, every thirty miles or so to allow your fast conveyance across France, to Calais."

"King Francis has no love for the

English," Tom Wyatt demurs. "He might well have us all arrested, and thrown into a dungeon."

"Nonsense!" the Doge says, heartily. "Cousin Francis is most enamoured of you English, at the moment. He believes that Thomas Cromwell still wishes to give him a one hundred thousand pound bribe, to buy his illegitimate daughter for the Medici dog."

"You doubt it will ever happen?" Tom Wyatt asks. It is his duty to find out what he can for Cromwell, and he suspects that there are plots within plots, throughout the whole of Italy.

"Alessandro has a perfectly delightful mistress, and he has also been promised to Emperor Charles' daughter, by Clement. The Pope is in a cleft stick, you see. He must stay friends with the emperor, and abandon his desire to be allied to Paris. The man has out thought himself."

"Then I pray we are safe home, before Francis realises he has been duped." Tom Wyatt bows, and leaves the Doge's presence, for the final time. He doubts he will ever return to Italy, and doubts that he would ever wish to.

Once out in the sunlit piazza of San Marco, the Englishman will make his way to the house of Alana Ipolatto, the newly widowed wife of Giovanni. He has the man's share of the campaign spoils, amounting to almost a hundred ducats, which will keep Alana and her child until she can remarry in a years time.

"We Venetians are a practical bunch," Bartolommeo explains to his English friend. "Once mourning is finished, a dozen young men will be knocking at her door. She is still only twenty two, and has a small fortune to bring to any new marriage."

"What of love?" The poet in Tom Wyatt is a little offended by so mercenary an approach to the business.

"You cannot eat love, *Tomas*," the Doge's nephew replies, sagely.

*

The swift galley, from Genoa to Marseilles is the gentle precursor to a long, twenty day ride up to the English stronghold of Calais, where the four strong party report to the English governor of the outpost.

"News of your coming has caused much activity between London and Calais, Captain Draper," the governor says, offering Will a refill of strong red wine. "The king commands that you take ship, whatever the weather in the channel, and go to him, at Whitehall Palace. I gather he is excited by the progress made by yourself, and Master Wyatt."

"We but delivered a message to the Bishop of Rome, sir," Will replies. "Now, we return with nothing more than his answer."

"But such an answer," the governor says. "Though it is not yet common knowledge, the Pope's refusal to grant an annulment is set to shake the world. I hear that Henry is already calling himself 'the defender of the faith', and strutting about as if he were already married to La Boleyn, and his poor wife put aside."

"I am sympathetic to the Dowager Princess of Wales' plight, sir, but it is her own stubbornness that creates most of her difficulties." Will has little time for political intrigues, but has been taught the basic responses by Thomas Cromwell.

"There are those who wish to trip us up," he preaches to his young men, "and we must be ever on guard." Then he will ask an opinion, and refine your views, so as to avoid causing offence to any, save the king's enemies.

"Of course," the governor replies, hurriedly altering his stance. Draper is a Cromwell man, and, until recently, the governor has been on cordial terms with the Lord Chancellor. "Your master has my fullest support, sir."

"I am sure he has," Tom Wyatt says, strolling into the elegantly furnished room. "For Master Cromwell's views are in line with the king's, and Henry thinks for the entire realm. What news from England, sir? Is More still bragging of how he has Clement's ear? Does the Bishop of Winchester still balance on his high wall, wondering which way to leap?"

"The Lord Chancellor still holds his office, but I fear the king pays little heed to him, since Master Cromwell's success in goading His Holiness into denying the king's will. I worry for our future, Master Wyatt."

"And Stephen Gardiner?" Will Draper asks. He knows that the man was a close friend of Cromwell's, and still has his master's sympathy, if nothing else. "I trust he is keeping to himself in Winchester?"

"The bishop seems to be quite close to His Majesty again," the governor replies. "I believe he is providing ecclesiastical support for the king, as Master Cromwell gives him legal, and judicial advice."

"Wise fellow," Tom Wyatt says, sarcastically. "Let me extemporise…" The poet thinks for a moment, then begins to recite.

'Watch carefully now,
the bishop creep,
to fawn and bow,
his lord to keep.

O, decisive fellow,
With his canon law,
Doth now mellow,
T'wards the whore.

"Dear Christ, man!" the governor cries, looking swiftly about the room. "What possesses you that you should even think such a thought, let alone write it down!"

"Come sir, we are all friends here," Tom Wyatt says, smiling at his two companions. "What think you of my little poem, sir?"

"Amusing, no doubt," the man replies. "You might recite it as you mount the scaffold. Why, the king will have you drawn, and quartered for this. You mad fool."

"You would tell on me?" The poet looks perplexed. "But you love the old queen, and mistrust Anne Boleyn, sir."

"Perhaps, but I love my country more, and if divorce, and remarriage will keep England from civil strife, I am for the king."

"Well said, sir," Will Draper says, finishing his wine. "You were the last task on our list, and we can now sail for England."

"I, a task?" The governor is confused.

"Master Wyatt was charged with testing your loyalty, sir," Will Draper replies. "Had you shown any lack of loyalty, we were to report it to our master."

"Dear God, Cromwell suspects me?"

"No longer," Will tells the white faced diplomat. "Rest assured, both Tom and I shall vouch for you. Though a small gift to my master might not go amiss. He is very fond of Flemish silverware, and a set of nicely engraved chargers will make him think fondly of you."

*

"Never do that to me again, Tom," Will says, as they leave the governor's house. "The man would have denounced you at the first opportunity. What possessed you … I mean to say … the Boleyn whore!"

"Forgive me, friend," Tom Wyatt replies with a sigh, "but my tongue often betrays my brain in matters of love."

"Love?" Will is unsure what love has to do with Wyatt's wicked little ditty.

He runs it through his mind again, and can see nothing but a sly dig at Gardiner, and a rude reference to the future queen of England.

"Aye, Will… love. *For what man can ever win, the love of she, my sweet Boleyn.*"

"That's enough!" Will takes his friend by the shoulder, and shakes him, hard. "There are enough slanders going about without you adding fuel to the fire."

"Slanders?" Tom Wyatt laughs then; a wild unnerving laugh, that speaks volumes to Will Draper. "Tell me, my friend, when once you have sipped of that sweet Italian wine, how can you return to rough French red, or common ale?"

"Will you shut up, Tom?" Will replies. "Or must I have Richard come and knock you senseless?"

"What's this?" Richard Cromwell saunters towards them, with Mush at his elbow. They have been wandering the dirty, shabbier parts of Calais. "I'll gladly bang Tom's head against a wall, but for what reason?"

"Don't tell me," Mush groans. "Master Wyatt is madly in love with the Lady Anne, and wishes to spout out his undying love to her."

"Do not jest about it," Will hisses. "If the king hears anymore about

323

Anne and Tom, he will demand an enquiry be made, and that can only end badly."

"She bids me come to her," the poet says, almost groaning. "Then, one might touch her hand, and receive a smile. Later she allows more. The flash of an ankle, or the swell of a bosom. I try to blot her from my mind, with other women. So many others. But no, she is my muse."

"She will be your executioner," Will retorts, sharply. "You cannot return to England, until the lady is safely married."

"Why cannot I have my love?" Tom Wyatt mutters. "*Though the stars grow cold* … ugh!" Richard Cromwell slips the leather covered cosh back up his sleeve and, without any real effort, throws the unconscious poet over one shoulder.

"One of my uncle's ships is in the harbour, bound for Portugal," he explains. "It is not a permanent solution, but it will keep him out of England for a couple of months."

"Then let us pray it is long enough," Mush says. "For nothing will keep me from my Gwen, and Miriam holds Will's heart. I would cross a burning desert to be with my love."

"Jesus!" Richard Cromwell says,

grinning at his dearest friends. "Everyone wants to be a bloody poet!"

~*end*~

Postscript

Though ***The Condottiero*** *is, essentially, a work of fiction, the story has a solid grounding in fact, and intertwines many real characters from the period. Where a real person is used, I try to keep them 'in character', and have them act within the constraints of the age. The condotta were bands of mercenary soldiers, who would contract themselves out to the various city states of Italy, and fight under strict rules of engagement. To break a contract, was to destroy a condottiero's honour, and make him a pariah amongst his fellow mercenaries.*

Thomas Cromwell *was, by late 1531, a prime mover in court politics, and was replacing the Lord Chancellor in Henry's mind, as the man who could deal with Rome. There is evidence to show that* emissaries from King Henry to Pope Clement were active from 1526 onwards, and it is more than likely that Cromwell was proactive with the Papal see from 1531 onwards. The Pope's refusal to annul Henry's marriage came in 1532, but would have been discussed within the Pope's circle earlier.

Rafe Sadler is Cromwell's right hand man. Born in 1507, he was by his mid twenties, a firm favourite with the Privy Councillor, and was often on hand when Cromwell spoke with the king. Portraits show him to be a ginger haired young man, with a fashionable pointed beard.

Thomas Wendy was a renowned physician at the court of the king, and often in his presence. He would have been a valued source of information to the likes of Eustace Chapuys.

Eustace Chapuys was the Emperor Charles' ambassador to England during the crisis over the king's wish for an annulment. He is often described as dapper, and a small, thin faced sort of a man. His wish to do the best he can for Queen Katherine is well documented, but he does not attach any blame to Henry. In a letter to his master, Chapuys was to write: 'The King himself is not ill-natured; it is this Anne who has put him in this perverse and wicked temper, and alienates him from his former humanity.' His ambassadorial residence was next to Austin Friars, and he was a close friend of Thomas Cromwell.

Pope Clement was a member of the infamous Medici family, and was noted for his corruption, and political infamies. He is considered a prime mover, with the Holy Roman Emperor, against the city state of Florence, which was captured after an Italian soldier of fortune, the condottiero, Malatesta Baglioni turned traitor. There is evidence that Clement made several attempts to marry his illegitimate son **Alessandro Medici** into one of the various royal families of the time, and was not above bribery and corruption to gain his ends.

Alessandro Medici became the Duke of Florence in 1532, after taking the city in 1531. It is now widely accepted that he was the son of a black African servant girl, and the man who was to become Pope Clement. He kept one lover for the whole of his short life, despite marrying Margaret of Austria, the *illegitimate daughter of Charles V.*

Considered by many to be one of the worst of the Medici family, Alessandro, known as il Moro, because of his 'Moorish' skin tone was suspected of poisoning his own brother, and finally died at the hands of an assassin, on January 6th 1537.

Tom Wyatt, *apart from being an up and coming poet at this time, was a roving ambassador for the English court, and spent long periods of time in France, and Italy. He was once an assistant to Lord Bedford, emissary to Rome in 1526/27.*

Stephen Gardiner *was, primarily a lawyer, specialising in church matters, who gained the confidence of King Henry. After spells in France, as a negotiator, he returned to England, where he was made into the Bishop of Winchester, at Henry's insistence. Noted for sitting on the political wall, Gardiner swapped allegiances several times, dependant on the king's moods.*

Thomas More *struggled to reconcile his political life with his religious beliefs, and managed to upset all the major players in the 'annulment'* *game. By the end of 1531, his career was on a knife edge, and he was being edged into early retirement. Though he clung on to the Lord Chancellorship for a few more months, Anne Boleyn was intent on his downfall. Thomas Cromwell seems to have played a rather passive part in More's removal, though he was active in the Lord Chancellor's eventual downfall.*

***Thomas Audley**, born in 1488 is, at this time, Speaker of the House of Commons, and a trusted advisor to the king, and his inner circle of friends. He was a friend of Cromwell's and finds advancement because of his support.*

***Richard Cromwell** was the nephew of Thomas, and worked alongside him in various capacities. I have taken some liberties with his general strength, and hearty character, but his various biographies describe him as 'tough' and 'hard', and state that he held an unswerving loyalty, and devotion for his uncle. In later years, he spent some time in the military. He was the son of Thomas Cromwell's sister, and changed his name from Williams, to Cromwell when he joined his uncles household.*

***Malatesta Baglioni** was a*

notorious condottiero, infamous for his betrayal of the Florentine Republic to the Medici family, and Charles V. He was born in 1491, and died in December, 1531, by which time he was the lord of Perugia, Bettona, and Spello, in Umbria.

He was the son of Gian Paolo Baglioni, ruler of Perugia, and Ippolita Conti. By the age of fifteen the precocious young man was made Count of Bettona. Later, during the brutal Italian Wars, he served the Republic of Venice, capturing the cities of Lodi, and Cremona. In 1527 he was lord of Perugia, after eliminating his brother, and then his uncle.

Contracted out to assume the defence of the Republic of Florence, the condottiero broke his solemn vow, and connived with Pope Clement VII, and the Imperial forces to betray the city. His treason was revealed on 3rd August 1530, at the Battle of Gavinana, in which the Florentine force, under Francesco Ferrucci was utterly destroyed by the Imperial army. Ferrucci's distraught exclamation 'Ahi traditor Malatesta!' has remained a famous remark in Italian culture. Baglioni was then able to return to Perugia in September, 1530. Once uncovered, as a traitor, his only friend would have been the Pope, which lends credence to my fiction of a Venetian invasion plot. He was in Umbria during the period of my story and, after a colourful life, died there at the end of the year 1531.

Andrea Gritti *was born in 1455. He was the Doge of Venice from 1523 to 1538, following a distinguished diplomatic, and military career. He was born in Bardolino, near Verona, but spent much of his early life in Constantinople, working as a grain merchant, and looking after Venetian political interests. By 1510, after some bad military reverses, he was put in charge of the Venetian armed forces, and recaptured Padua and Verona from the Emperor's clutches.*

Recognised as one of the city's greatest ever Doges, he continued to intrigue against Venice's many enemies, with some success. He died in December 1538, at the age of eighty three!

San Gemini *is a small municipality of about 5000 inhabitants, in the province of Terni in the Italian region of Umbria, located about 35 miles south of Perugia, and about 6 miles northwest of Terni. The town is a well-preserved medieval burgh with two lines of walls, built over the remains of a small Roman outpost, along the old Via Flaminia. The action I describe, is fictional.*

Edward Wotton *Born in 1492, Wotton became a noted physician, and is acknowledged as one of the first truly great zoologists. He was widely travelled, and a friend of the Duke of Norfolk. He was in Venice at the period of this story, and I can only apologise to his shade for intimating that he was a spy, in the pay of Thomas Cromwell.*

Ignatius Loyola *became the founding father of the Jesuit movement in later years, but spent the period before, travelling Europe, looking for men of character, who wished to become God's soldiers. I have no evidence that puts him in Italy at this time, but his travels took him, time and again, to Paris, Rome and Venice. Once again, I apologise to him for making him into something he may not have been.*

Lodovico Falier and Mario Savorgnano, *though minor characters in the story, both existed. Lodovico was the Venetian ambassador to the court of King Henry at this time, and the splendidly named Mario Savorgnano is mentioned in court papers, as a Venetian gentleman, 'travelling for pleasure'.*

My apologies to Thomas Wyatt for putting poetry into his mouth, which I wrote, and which lacks his style. My only excuse is that I am a fiction writer, and must use some devices to move the story along.

Thank you for choosing this book from our catalogue of exclusive to Amazon titles. Here are some of our other titles, which may be of further reading interest. TightCircle is a small, independent publishers, and is supported entirely by customer sales, or rentals. If you like what you read, please tell your friends.

Printed in Great Britain
by Amazon

39449011R00199